THE PINK WEDDING DRESS WHODUNIT

PARANORMAL COZY MYSTERY

A WITCH'S COVE MYSTERY
BOOK NINETEEN

VELLA DAY

EROTIC READS PUBLISHING

Copyright © 2023 Vella Day

www.velladay.com

velladayauthor@gmail.com

Edited by Rebecca Cartee

ALL RIGHTS RESERVED. No part of this book may be used or reproduced in any manner whatsoever without written permission of the author except in the case of brief questions embodied in critical articles or reviews.

This is a work of fiction. Names, characters, places, and incidents either are the product of the author's imagination or are used fictitiously, and any resemblance to actual persons living or dead, business establishments, events or locales, is entirely coincidental.

ABOUT THE BOOK

My wedding was perfect--until it wasn't. A lost ring and a dead body could ruin even the happiest of days.

Picture this: I, Glinda Goodall, soon to be Glinda Harrison, was standing at the altar, moments away from saying "I do." And that's when it happened. In the midst of the ceremony, my faithful companion, Iggy, a talking pink iguana and my trusted familiar, managed to misplace the ring. How, you ask? Well, in the process of investigating the shocking discovery of a lifeless body beneath a church pew, he accidentally swallowed the ring. Talk about wedding day drama!

Naturally, the wedding had to be postponed. Although I admit I was disappointed, my priority quickly shifted to retrieving the ring from Iggy and, of course, uncovering the truth behind the murder. No worries, though—I was prepared for the challenge. After all, my fiancé, Jaxson, and I are the proprietors of an amateur sleuth business, always ready to dive headfirst into a perplexing mystery.

So, if you find yourself in Witch's Cove, don't hesitate to

drop by and check on our progress. Join us as we unravel the enigma surrounding the demise of the antique dealer. And who knows? When the time finally comes, I might extend a personal invitation for you to witness our wedding—whenever that may be.

CHAPTER 1

I, Glinda Goodall, a not-very-powerful witch, stood before the mirror in my cozy bedroom, fidgeting with the delicate pink skirt of my wedding dress. Aunt Fern's skilled hands had fashioned this gown with love. As she gently tugged at the fabric, I could feel the warmth of her affection radiating from her. However, despite her meticulous attention to every seam, I found it impossible to stand still as my thoughts raced.

"Stop moving. If I didn't know better, I'd say you didn't want to marry Jaxson," Aunt Fern said, her voice laced with concern.

Her comment startled me. "That's the most ridiculous thing you could say. I adore Jaxson. We are absolutely perfect for each other."

Aunt Fern placed her hands gently on my shoulders, locking her gaze with mine. "Then what is it, dear?"

I sighed, my eyes shifting toward Iggy, my pink iguana familiar, who was lounging on the bed nearby. "You still have the ring, right?" I asked, my worry seeping into my voice.

While I trusted Iggy implicitly to be the ring bearer, his tendency to become distracted gave me pause.

With a hip-swinging crawl, Iggy descended from the bed, his tiny lizard feet padding softly against the floor. Clutched tightly in his mouth was the ring, an heirloom from Jaxson's family. He placed it on the floor. "Will you relax? You're making me nervous." Iggy's voice was tinged with exasperation.

And yes, Iggy possessed the uncanny ability to talk. There were moments when I wished he would keep his chatter to a minimum, especially when my mind was preoccupied.

"I'm sorry, Iggy," I murmured. My gaze flitted toward the clock on the wall. Only ten minutes remained until my parents would be parked outside to drive us to the church.

Rolling his eyes, Iggy glanced at the ring. "This isn't going anywhere but on your finger. Now quit your fretting before I change my mind about being your best man."

My gasp was audible even though I suspected he was kidding—or at least I hoped he was. Iggy had been my steadfast companion for as long as I could remember. He wouldn't dream of missing this momentous occasion.

"You wouldn't!" I exclaimed.

A glint danced in Iggy's eyes as he leaned closer. "Try me," he whispered, teasingly wagging his tail.

Despite the lingering uncertainty, a smile tugged at the corners of my lips. Iggy's playful antics had a way of soothing my nerves.

I took a deep breath, feeling a surge of excitement mingle with the tinge of nervous anticipation. It was time to embrace the magic of the day and trust that everything would fall into place. After all, between Aunt Fern's craftsmanship, Iggy's mischievous loyalty, and the most amazing man waiting for me at the altar, how could anything go wrong?

Penny Carsted, my closest friend, would stand by my side as my maid of honor, and Jaxson's brother, Drake, would be Jaxson's best man. My mom said she'd rather watch from the pews than be dressed up on the altar. Who was I to say no?

To avoid Iggy's inevitable protest, we decided to humorously declare him my best man. After all, the thought of him throwing a fit on such a momentous day was inconceivable.

As I glanced at the ribbon laid out on my vanity, a good idea crossed my mind. "You know, Iggy, maybe I should tie the ring around your neck, just to be safe."

Iggy snorted, clearly not amused. "Don't even think about it. If you had chosen a child to carry the ring, you wouldn't tie it around their neck. You'd sew it onto a pillow or something equally absurd."

He had a point. I took a deep breath as my hands smoothed over the exquisite pink dress. "Today simply has to be perfect."

Aunt Fern fussed over the dress for another few minutes, her attention to detail evident in every adjustment. Finally, a warm smile graced her lips as she patted my arm. "You look lovely, dear. Absolutely gorgeous." She then pulled out her phone. "I'll call your dad and let him know we're a few minutes early."

A mixture of excitement and nerves churned in my stomach, a tangible reminder that this was truly going to be our day.

"Okay," Aunt Fern said and then disconnected. "They're already downstairs."

"Of course they are."

Scooping Iggy into my arms, the three of us descended the stairs and made our way to the side entrance to Coven's Pathway where my parents were parked at the curb.

My father practically leaped out of the car, his eyes brimming with emotion. "Oh, my. Glinda, you look breathtaking."

His voice wavered, hinting at the emotions bubbling just beneath the surface. Since I was his only child, I could understand his reaction.

If my dad started to cry, I knew I would quickly follow suit. "Thank you, Dad."

"Are you ready?" he asked, his voice filled with a mixture of pride and tenderness.

I offered a soft smile, bracing myself for the magical journey ahead. "As ready as I'll ever be."

With Aunt Fern's assistance, I settled into the backseat. My mom turned around, her eyes filled with awe. "Glinda, you look stunning. Fern, the dress is incredible." From her purse, my mom produced what appeared to be a garter. "Slide this on under your dress."

I held it up, finding Glinda the Good Witch's face smiling back at me—an homage to the Wizard of Oz. "Really, Mom?"

She shrugged, a glint in her eye. "You needed something blue. It was the best I could do."

I couldn't help but chuckle. My mom's dedication to all things related to that iconic movie extended even to our family's funeral home, where a long yellow runner honored the yellow brick road. In her own quirky way, she added a touch of whimsy to our special day.

The drive to the church was blissfully short despite the streets of Witch's Cove teeming with activity. Half the town seemed to be attending our wedding, while the other half dutifully minded their beloved shops. Being in a Florida beach town, the perpetual flow of tourists never ceased.

When we arrived, a gasp escaped my lips. The quaint church had been transformed into a haven of elegance, adorned with cascading tulle and lace, delicate pink roses, and sprigs of baby's breath. And that was just the outside of the church. I couldn't imagine what the inside looked like.

"The gossip queens truly have outdone themselves this

time," Iggy mumbled after removing the ring from his mouth for a moment. He peered out the window with his keen eyes.

His remark struck true. Maude and Miriam Daniels, the spirited elderly twins who owned the coffee and tea shops in town, had done the handiwork. Aunt Fern mentioned that Dolly Andrews, the lively proprietor of the local diner, and Pearl Dillsmith, the efficient sheriff's dispatcher, had lent their artistic touch to the decorations as well.

"Let's get this show on the road before I change my mind about being involved in this wedding shindig," Iggy stated.

Sheesh. He acted as if he was the one in charge. Wanting him to be happy and focused, I didn't reply. With a gentle touch, I lifted Iggy from the backseat and placed him on the ground. Since he was always eager to check things out, Iggy preferred to explore his surroundings himself rather than be carried.

The resounding peal of the church bells filled the air, and my heart swelled with joy.

Aunt Fern received a text. "It's time, dear. Jaxson is waiting to marry you."

Drawing in a deep breath. "Let's do this," I mumbled to myself.

Casting a final glance at Iggy to ensure he had the ring securely in his mouth, I grabbed my dad's arm. Jaxson would be at the altar, and our dear friends, filled with love and anticipation, would be seated in the pews.

My mother and Aunt Fern headed inside to take their seats, eager to witness my walk down the aisle. As my dad and I—and Iggy—entered the church, the majestic notes of the organ swelled, resounding through the air. A hushed breath escaped as I studied all of the various shades of pink that adorned the end of the pews and the altar. There was even a soft pink runner on the aisle.

At that moment, I felt surrounded by an overwhelming

sense of love. Aunt Fern's group of gossip queens were sitting together, their supportive presence very welcome.

My handsome fiancé stood at the altar, exuding charm in his dashing black tuxedo. And yes, a pink hibiscus was in his lapel, a nod to my love for the color and a delightful tribute to Iggy's favorite food.

As my father and I slowly glided down the aisle, all my worries faded into insignificance. In that precious instant, nothing else mattered. This was our moment to embark on a future filled with love, laughter, and enchantment!

Upon reaching the altar, a smile graced my lips as I glanced at Penny, my steadfast maid of honor, and then at my lovely bridesmaids. Though not everyone I had wished to be present could attend, their absence was due to the demands of their own cherished stores that needed tending.

As soon as our vows were exchanged, I turned around to signal Iggy, our ring bearer, to present us with the ring. However, my heart skipped a beat when I realized he was nowhere to be found. My gaze sought out Jaxson, my soon-to-be husband, who remained remarkably composed.

"Iggy?" Jaxson's gentle yet firm voice carried with it a touch of concern.

In the next instant, Iggy poked his head out from one of the vacant pews at the end of the aisle and then waddled his way toward us. Whispers began to ripple through the congregation as their eyes fell upon my familiar. It was then that it struck me—he didn't have the ring.

"Iggy! Where is the ring?" My words betrayed my calmer intentions.

"I, uh, swallowed it," Iggy confessed when he finally reached us. He sounded genuinely embarrassed.

"You did what?" I exclaimed, my composure slipping.

"I was so startled that I accidentally swallowed it." Iggy's words rushed together.

Jaxson swiftly scooped up my familiar, my fiancé's expression a mix of curiosity and concern. "What startled you, Iggy?"

"The dead body," Iggy replied.

Only those with the gift of magic could hear Iggy speak, and few were near enough to catch his revelation, though I was sure many noticed my open mouth and wide-open eyes. "A dead body? You actually saw a dead body?" My hands began to tremble.

"Yes," Iggy confirmed.

Curiosity and worry intermingled as I turned to face the bewildered congregation.

Before I could address the attendees, Jaxson stepped into the church aisle. "I apologize, but we need to postpone the wedding." Gasps of disbelief echoed through the church. "There's nothing to worry about. Glinda and I are still getting married, just not at this moment," he quickly reassured everyone. "It seems as if Iggy has accidentally swallowed the ring. We apologize for the inconvenience. If all of you could kindly exit the church in an orderly manner, we would appreciate it. Don't worry. The Tiki Hut Grill has been reserved for our wedding reception. There's no reason why you can't all enjoy the amazing food Fern has prepared. Glinda and I need to attend to Iggy. I'm sure you understand."

Jaxson had handled the situation with class. I was glad he didn't say something about the dead body. That would have caused a real mess.

I hoped that when the ladies decorated the church last night, the body wasn't present. Otherwise, they might have compromised some of the forensic evidence.

I lifted my hand and waved. "Ah, Sheriff Rocker? Could you and Nash please stay behind?" I was aware of the mounting confusion among our guests, but that couldn't be helped.

As the crowd dispersed, their expression was filled with curiosity and concern. I then turned to the preacher who was conducting the ceremony.

His eyes held a compassionate understanding. "Glinda, Jaxson, when would you like to reschedule?" he inquired, offering us a moment to regroup and plan for our postponed wedding day.

"Soon," I assured him. "Hopefully, very soon."

CHAPTER 2

Despite our efforts to clear the wedding venue and allow only the sheriff and his deputy to remain, my parents, Aunt Fern, and Jaxson's parents, along with most of the wedding party stayed behind.

"Did Iggy really swallow the ring, or is something else going on?" my mother asked.

Taking a deep breath, I knew it was time to reveal the truth. "Iggy did swallow the ring, but it happened because he discovered a dead body in the back of the church," I admitted, knowing that the secret would inevitably surface.

Jaxson's parents—especially his mom—were totally shocked.

"Mom, Dad, let's go outside," Jaxson suggested.

Drake placed a hand on his brother's arm. "You stay here. I'll see that they keep out of the way."

Jaxson nodded. "Appreciate it."

"So there won't be a wedding today?" His mom's eyes watered.

"Maddie, we are still getting married," I assured Jaxson's mother. "Just not today. I mean, we could get married without the ring, but having a dead body in the church is kind of a downer, don't you think? And I have to make sure Iggy is okay."

"You're right, of course." His mother hugged me and then brushed a few errant strands of my hair out of my face. "Take good care of him."

I assumed she meant Jaxson, though she could have meant Iggy. "I will."

As soon as Drake ushered his parents outside, Penny stepped next to me. "If you need any help, I'm here for you."

I hugged her. "I know. Thank you."

"Call me. You know I like to hear every detail," she said.

Since Penny was a witch who was quite good at knowing if a person was lying, she would be a valuable person to have on this investigation—assuming the person had been murdered and some sort of witchcraft had been involved. "I will."

No sooner had my maid of honor, along with the rest of the wedding party, left the church than Sheriff Rocker, our competent sheriff, approached.

One of the perks of having him as our sheriff was that I had managed to cast a spell on him, as well as on Jaxson, enabling them to communicate with Iggy. Strangely, the spell hadn't worked on Deputy Nash.

"Glinda, what's all this about?" Sheriff Rocker inquired.

I glanced down at Iggy, silently urging him to show us what he had found. My parents, being owners of the local funeral home, were no strangers to encountering dead bodies, so I didn't ask them to leave.

"Follow me." Iggy waddled down the aisle, and I could only imagine the exaggerated tale he would weave for his friends about this unexpected discovery. Knowing him, he would probably claim to have solved the crime within a matter of minutes.

As the entourage marched down the aisle, I prayed it wasn't someone I knew.

"I found a dead body under this pew," Iggy declared proudly, his eyes gleaming with accomplishment and mischief.

Clad in my wedding gown, I wasn't in the best position to drop to my knees and check it out. That was the sheriff's job, after all. Both Sheriff Rocker and Deputy Nash crouched down to examine the space under the pew seat. After a moment, the sheriff rose.

"It's Harold Hastings," he announced, his voice tinged with surprise.

My shock was palpable. Harold Hastings, an eccentric but seemingly harmless elderly man who ran an antique shop in town was the body under the pew? How terrible. While I had always suspected he had magical abilities, our interactions had been too infrequent for me to confirm it.

"How did he die?" I questioned.

"I'm not the medical examiner," he replied, evading the answer with practiced ease.

Knowing the sheriff wouldn't divulge any further details, Deputy Nash stepped forward, breaking the tense silence. "I'll call Dr. Sanchez," he offered, taking charge of the necessary next steps.

I had so many questions, but they could wait. Hastings wasn't going anywhere—until Elissa came, that is. In the meantime, I needed to see to Iggy. I turned to my familiar. "How are you feeling?"

"Okay. It's not like I can feel the ring inside me or anything."

"Are you sure you swallowed it? Could you have dropped it?"

Iggy looked over at Jaxson. "It's not too late to back out, you know."

"Don't be snarky. It's a legit question," I said.

"Fine. I know I swallowed it."

I could take Iggy to a vet to see about getting it out, but Dr. Nichols might suggest waiting to see if it passed. Trust me, the ring was too big for that. Once they realized the severity of the situation, he might suggest operating, and that was not something I wanted to put my familiar through.

Jaxson stepped closer. "How about seeing if Andorra can at least confirm the ring is inside him?"

Andorra worked at the Hex and Bones Apothecary and was Drake's girlfriend. "She can only tell what poison a person might have ingested. No, we need Dr. Sanchez to X-ray him."

"I think she's going to be too busy to do that," Jaxson said.

"Then we'll go to Gertrude," I announced.

"How can Gertrude help?" he asked.

Gertrude Poole was our most powerful witch in Witch's Cove. She might be in her nineties, but she still had talent. "I'm hoping she can use some kind of magic to remove it."

"I thought she wasn't feeling well," he said. "It's why she didn't come to the wedding."

"Between you and me, I don't think Gertrude likes the ceremony of it all. Worst case, we take him to Levy." Levy Poole was Gertrude's grandson; he ran a coven in a nearby town. His group had a library of spells that would rival anyone's. They'd know which spells might do the trick.

Iggy looked up at me, his eyes wide with fear. "What if they can't get it out?"

I knelt down next to him and stroked his back. "Don't worry; we'll figure it out."

As we waited for Dr. Sanchez, I couldn't help but wonder who could have wanted to harm the old man. As far as I knew, he didn't have any enemies. And even if he did, why kill him now? Or was I getting ahead of myself? Since Jaxson and I ran the Pink Iguana Sleuths Agency, I had a tendency to think all deaths were a result of murder.

My thoughts were interrupted by the sound of Elissa's heels clicking on the floor as she rushed into the chapel. "I'm so sorry, Glinda, that this had to happen on your wedding day. What a nightmare."

"Thanks. Given the circumstances, I'm glad that Rihanna didn't cancel her photography job on the cruise ship to come home for the wedding." Rihanna was my twenty-year-old niece, who happened to be dating Elissa's son. We'd invited Elissa, of course, but she, too, had work obligations.

"Given how it turned out, I'm glad too," the medical examiner stated.

"Before you look at the body, can you check Iggy? He swallowed our ring by mistake."

"I deal with dead people, you know."

Iggy waddled up to Dr. Sanchez. "I'm not dead yet, but I might be soon if someone doesn't get this out of me." Yes, Iggy loved being dramatic. Unfortunately, the medical examiner couldn't understand him.

"Can you at least feel his body to see if the ring is indeed inside?" Jaxson asked.

"It's inside," Iggy said.

Dr. Sanchez sighed. "I could do an ultrasound, but other than cutting the ring out of him, I can't do much. What about Dr. Nichols? He's a vet."

"We might have to go that route."

"Doc," the sheriff said. "We do have a dead body here."

Whoops. "Go take care of Harold. I'll be curious to know how he died."

"I hope to find that out soon."

Iggy protested loudly as I carried him out to the car. I held him on my lap while Jaxson drove us to the clinic. Iggy was squirming and whining the whole way there.

"I thought we were going to see Gertrude," he complained. "I bet she can get it out."

"It's possible, but let's confirm with Dr. Nicols there isn't an easy way to remove it. Okay?"

"Fine. If you didn't know, Mr. Hastings is a warlock."

"Really? How do you know?"

"Hugo told me."

"And Hugo would know." Iggy's best friend was a mute gargoyle shifter with many hidden talents, one of which was his ability to communicate telepathically with Iggy. What I wouldn't give to be able to do that with Jaxson? "Thanks for the info."

Once we arrived at the vet's office, Dr. Nichols took Iggy into the exam room while Jaxson and I waited in the reception area. After what felt like hours, Dr. Nichols emerged, looking grim.

"The ring is lodged in his esophagus. I'm sorry, but we're going to have to do surgery to remove it."

"We have a friend who might have a more...natural way," I explained.

The doctor shrugged. "Suit yourself, but don't take too long. No telling what might happen if it shifts deeper inside him."

Iggy, who had been in the examination room, waddled out. "Get me out of here," he protested.

Thankfully, the vet couldn't understand him either. Jaxson quickly picked up Iggy. Once I paid for the vet's services, we left.

"Let's go see Gertrude," I said. "She's our best bet now."

"We should have gone there first," Iggy complained.

"In hindsight, you might be right."

Gertrude's cottage was on the outskirts of town. Her place was small and unassuming, but I knew the inside was filled with powerful magic.

We knocked, and within seconds, Gertrude answered. Being a psychic, I suspected she already knew we were on the way, even though Gertrude claimed that wasn't how her talent worked.

"Oh, my, but this is a surprise," she said as she motioned us inside. "And so handsome too. Congratulations on your nuptials."

"We didn't get married," I said. "Yet."

Her cheeks sagged. "Come in and tell me everything."

The living room was heavily scented with lavender and rosemary, which reminded me of Gertrude's office in town.

I explained that Iggy had swallowed the wedding ring because he had been startled seeing a dead body under the pew.

"That would startle me too. Do you know who died?" Gertrude asked.

"Harold Hastings."

"Harold? Oh, what a shame. He seemed like such a nice man."

"Iggy says he was a warlock," I said.

"He was, and from what I was able to sense, quite a powerful one too," Gertrude explained.

"I'm surprised I've not heard of him performing any spells or anything." I had lived in Witch's Cove my whole life, though Harold had only moved to town a few years back.

"He mentioned he had a bad experience or two with some of his fellow warlocks. Harold said he wanted to put that part of his life in the past."

That was an interesting piece of information. If Iggy wasn't in need of treatment, I would have continued picking her brain. "So, do you think you can help Iggy? The vet said the ring was lodged deep in his throat. Dr. Nichols wanted to operate, but I said I wanted to try other methods."

She smiled. "I'm glad you did." Gertrude lifted Iggy from

my arms. "You poor thing. Let's see about getting that nasty ring out."

Iggy turned back to me and stuck his little tongue out. He was a cheeky one. Iggy adored Gertrude. I sensed that he would work the sympathy angle for all it was worth.

"I hope I don't die first," Iggy said, followed by a moan.

Oh, boy.

Jaxson and I sat on the sofa while she held Iggy. I assumed Gertrude could use her intuition or magical ways to detect what was going on inside of him.

"Jaxson, in the cabinet over by the far wall is a basket full of my herbs. Be a dear and get it for me," Gertrude said.

Jaxson jumped up and retrieved it for her.

"What are you going to do?" Iggy asked.

"I plan to do a spell that will move the ring, but I need Glinda to use her telekinetic ability to move it where we want it to go," Gertrude said.

"I've been practicing my magic, but my ability to move things with my mind is a bit spotty."

"Nonsense, dear. I know you can do it. After all, you had the best teacher." Gertrude winked.

I had trained under Gertrude. "I'll do my best."

"Will it hurt?" Iggy asked.

Gertrude smiled. "Let's hope not."

Knowing how Gertrude liked to work, I lit several candles while she set out the bowls of herbs and incense. Once she mixed what was needed and lit the incense, she held Iggy.

"Glinda, while I recite the spell, concentrate on helping the ring move forward." Gertrude ran a loving hand over his head. "And you, mister, stay still. Glinda might need to reach in and take the ring."

"Or I can just spit it out once it moves," Iggy said.

"Whatever works." Gertrude looked up at me. "Ready?"

"Yes."

"Jaxson, please turn off the two lamps and close the shades. The darker, the better. It sets the mood," Gertrude said.

"Be happy to."

As soon as Jaxson did as he was asked, Gertrude closed her eyes. She inhaled and began her chant.

> *By the powers of mystic weave and craft,*
> *I seek to undo this peculiar draft.*
> *From within the body of this creature dear,*
> *Release the swallowed object without fear.*
> *Let the spell unfurl with magical might,*
> *Grant freedom from this unintended plight.*
> *With whispered words, I now decree,*
> *From the iguana's body, set it free.*

I WAS SO ENCHANTED by her words that I forgot my role in all of this. I quickly focused on moving the ring forward with my mind. Whether it was my magic or Gertrude's witchcraft at work, Iggy gagged. And that was when I saw the shiny gold object.

Iggy coughed and expelled the ring. It hit the table and rolled. While it was a bit slimy, I was thrilled that Iggy would no longer be at risk of choking.

"Thank goodness," I said.

Jaxson jumped up. "Let me clean it."

He grabbed the ring and disappeared into Gertrude's kitchen. The water ran and he then returned. "Good as new."

"Maybe you should put it in your pocket," I suggested.

"You don't trust me anymore?" Iggy asked.

"No," Jaxson and I said in unison.

"Fine." Iggy lifted his snout.

"Don't you have something to say to Gertrude?" I asked.

He turned around, crawled up her arm, and kissed her cheek. "Thank you."

She smiled. "You're very welcome." Gertrude looked at Iggy. "I'm sure you want to investigate the murder, but these spells can take a toll on a body. You'll need to rest for the day, young man."

"Yes, ma'am."

What? Iggy wasn't usually this polite. He must have something up his sleeve. Or in this case, it would be up his tuxedo sleeve.

I stood. "I can't thank you enough."

"Nonsense. You're the one who did it. My spell was merely to relax you."

Was that true? "Well, it worked."

She winked. "It was my lucky day. I got to visit with my favorite familiar and see you in your wedding dress."

Gertrude was the nicest woman. I couldn't help but lean over and hug her. "Thank you, again."

Once we climbed into the car, I relaxed. Iggy was safe, and the ring was back in our possession. "I hope the wedding guests went to Aunt Fern's place to eat all that food."

Jaxson started the car. "People from the wedding will be expecting the lavish reception. I bet they'll go to the Tiki Hut. It's not like we called off the wedding because we didn't want to get married."

"Let's hope you're right."

A few minutes later, Jaxson pulled up in front of the restaurant. "How about we change and then check to see if the sheriff has learned anything?"

CHAPTER 3

"I would normally jump at the chance to delve into the details of a potential murder," I remarked. "I know Steve will be eager to learn that Harold was a warlock—not that it necessarily had anything to do with his demise, but it might have."

Jaxson's eyebrows raised. "Normally?"

"I think we should make an appearance at our own wedding reception," I said. "In my mind, we are already married. The only things we haven't done are have the final kiss and sign some papers."

Leaning over, Jaxson gave me a tender kiss. "Now you have the kiss. Let's go."

A smile tugged at the corners of my lips. "I know some people will be worried about Iggy, and this will put their minds at ease to know he's all right. The rest will want reassurance that we fully intend to complete our wedding vows."

He waved a hand. "You're right. I wasn't thinking."

After Jaxson turned off the engine, he walked around to my side and opened the car door. The man was a gentleman. I carefully carried Iggy in my arms, well aware of the potential dangers posed by a bustling restaurant full of people. The last thing we needed was for someone to accidentally step on my beloved familiar.

As we entered the reception venue, the room erupted into applause. Raising my hand to quiet the crowd, I felt compelled to offer a brief explanation. "Good news. Iggy is fine. And we managed to retrieve the ring," I announced.

Jaxson slipped his hand into his pocket and held it up, triggering a flurry of questions about when we would proceed with the remainder of the ceremony. I confessed that I wasn't entirely sure yet. I wanted to discuss the possibility of a more intimate, private ceremony with Jaxson and our parents for the next go around. But for now, we would revel in the joyous atmosphere of the reception.

For the next hour, we mingled with our guests, exchanging warm conversations and well wishes. Eventually, we found our seats and savored the amazing meal that Aunt Fern's cooks had prepared. Everything was divine.

A few curious individuals inquired about the absence of the sheriff and his deputy. In response, I explained that they had been called away on an unexpected, last-minute case. Little did they know the true extent of the situation that had unfolded.

After delighting in cutting the cake and engaging in more lively chats with our guests, Jaxson, Iggy, and I finally retreated upstairs to our apartment.

"As pretty as it is, I can't wait to get out of this dress," I exclaimed, feeling the fabric constricting me.

"You? This tuxedo is itching me like crazy," Iggy chimed in, his scaly arms wriggling. "Please take it off me."

I chuckled. "My pleasure." With the assumption that Jaxson and I would be officially married by now, he had already moved most of his clothes into my apartment, allowing him to change as well. We had debated moving into

Jaxson's larger place, but mine was so convenient to our work and to the restaurant.

"How about we find out what Steve has learned?" Jaxson suggested.

"You read my mind."

"I need to go with you," Iggy interjected. "I was the only eyewitness, you know."

I raised an eyebrow. "An eyewitness is someone who actually saw Mr. Hastings die. Did you witness anything of that sort?"

"Not really," Iggy admitted.

I had to probe further. Iggy liked to say cryptic things, sometimes just for the shock value of it. "What does that mean? Did you see someone lurking or behaving suspiciously?" Considering that Iggy had entered the church behind my father and me, I doubted he had witnessed anything of significance.

"No, but I don't want to stay here alone. What if I suddenly develop symptoms and need help?"

"But how can you have any symptoms? The ring is no longer inside you."

"I know, but Gertrude mentioned something..." Iggy began, his voice trailing off.

I had to interrupt him. "Yes, that you need to rest, Iggy. Gertrude's orders."

"Fine. Then how about you take me downstairs to the party, just in case I encounter any problems?"

Understanding his apprehension about him not wanting to be alone, I nodded. "I'll take you downstairs. I think that's a good idea."

The three of us made our way back to the restaurant, rejoining the lively reception. Aunt Fern, spotting us with Iggy, approached us with curiosity etched on her face.

"What's going on? I thought you'd want to stay until the end of the reception."

"Normally, we would," I replied.

Aunt Fern's eyebrows arched, well aware of my penchant for investigating mysteries. "Don't tell me you're going to try to solve the case?"

"I thought Jaxson and I could inquire about Harold. He was a warlock, you know."

"I know," Aunt Fern acknowledged, leaning her elbows on the counter. "If you're diving into this investigation, assuming Harold was murdered, I suggest you look into Priscilla Primm."

"The writer?" I queried, intrigued by the unexpected lead.

"Aspiring writer," Aunt Fern corrected. "You know how I love antiques."

"I do," I replied.

Aunt Fern leaned over even closer, as if she didn't want anyone at the party to hear her. "Well, a few weeks ago, I was in Harold's shop, and who should be there but Priscilla Primm."

"You were there too. That doesn't make you a murderer."

Aunt Fern shook her head, her eyes gleaming. "No, but she expressed a keen interest in a book that Harold supposedly possessed."

Now, my curiosity was piqued. "What kind of book?"

"I'm not sure exactly. All I know is that Priscilla was convinced this book contained magical secrets," she said.

"Why would that be incriminating?" I asked.

"Everyone knows that Priscilla is desperate to sell her novel—a book she hasn't even finished, mind you. I overheard her telling Harold that if she had this book, she could write a bestseller."

I nodded. "I suppose that could be a motive, but until we

ascertain the cause of Harold's death, it would be premature to point fingers."

Aunt Fern's eyes sparkled. "That may be true, but remember, I gave you the idea, just in case it turns out to be her."

A smile played on my lips. "Thank you, Aunt Fern. I'll be sure to credit you if Priscilla is found guilty."

With Iggy safely entrusted to Aunt Fern's care, Jaxson and I stealthily slipped out through the side entrance, the late afternoon breeze embracing us as we ventured forth. "I know Steve won't have received any information from the medical examiner yet, but perhaps he's discovered some other evidence," I said.

Jaxson shrugged. "You can ask, but I'm willing to bet he won't divulge anything."

I mulled over the possibilities. "Perhaps Steve will be more forthcoming once I reveal that Harold was a warlock."

"Steve might leak information only if Harold was murdered—and not by conventional means."

"That's true." I know it sounded bad that I wished Harold had died at the hand of someone else, but we hadn't encountered an intriguing case in quite some time, and I yearned for the opportunity to sink my teeth into a captivating mystery. "If Steve won't cooperate or doesn't know anything, maybe we should let it go, at least for now."

Jaxson pulled me into a comforting embrace. "Glinda Goodall—soon to be Glinda Harrison—I know you too well. You couldn't possibly let this go any more than you could refuse to marry me."

I loved when he flirted with me. "Is that so?" I teased.

He placed a tender kiss on my nose. "That's so," he assured me.

"Then we need to find someone who can shed light on Harold's warlock tendencies."

Jaxson dipped his chin. "As I said, Harold being a warlock

may have nothing to do with his demise. He was, after all, an elderly man. Natural causes can't be ruled out."

I let out a sigh. "You're right. Let's proceed with caution and gather more information before drawing any firm conclusions." That's what Jaxson always said.

"A wise choice."

"I can't help but wonder how a person could have ended up under the pew if foul play wasn't the cause of death however. Do you think he was having a heart attack and crawled under the seat?" I asked.

Jaxson's brows furrowed. "That's a good question. He could have been in the church to pray, had a heart attack, fell forward, hit his head on the pew in front of him, and then collapsed onto the ground."

"Very possible, but that still doesn't explain how he ended up *under* the seat. He was completely hidden from view except from Iggy," I pointed out.

Jaxson snapped his fingers, a spark of realization crossing his face. "Maybe he was hiding from someone."

Suppressing a laugh, I remarked, "A grown man crawled under a seat to hide? An elderly one at that?"

"If someone was after him, he might resort to desperate measures," Jaxson suggested.

"Okay, I like that idea. But first, we need to learn how he died. If he hit his forehead and collapsed, he'd likely have a bruise on his face."

"Agreed, but since that information won't be available for a while, we should gather as much information as we can about Harold Hastings," Jaxson suggested.

I appreciated his quick thinking. "Who would know about him other than Gertrude? Do we know who his friends were?"

"I don't. My best bet would be someone at the Hex and Bones Apothecary might know. Even if Gertrude didn't think he practiced magic anymore, people talk. He might have visited the store, engaged in conversation, and possibly revealed something."

A playful remark escaped my lips. "You're so much more than just a pretty face."

Jaxson's cheeks flushed slightly. "At least call me handsome, but yes, I have my moments."

"To the Hex and Bones, then." I was determined to gather any clues that might shed light on Harold's life. We needed some ammunition to present to Steve so he'd let us help him with the investigation.

We crossed the street and entered the shop. To my delight, Bertha Murdoch, the owner, was present. Usually, her granddaughters, Andorra and Elizabeth, managed the store, but today, Bertha was there.

"What are you two doing here?" Bertha's surprise was understandable. "I thought you were getting married."

The news apparently hadn't reached her yet, or perhaps she pretended not to know. "We were—and we still are," I assured her, offering a brief explanation of Iggy swallowing the ring, his discovery of Harold Hastings's lifeless body, and Gertrude's assistance in retrieving the ring.

"Harold is dead?" Bertha's voice trembled.

"I'm afraid so."

Bertha shook her head. "Was it from a spell?"

My heart skipped a beat. Bertha's remark suggested she might possess crucial information. This was truly intriguing. "I don't have all the details yet. Elissa is examining the body. Harold was elderly, so it's possible he could have had a heart attack."

"Agreed, but you mentioned that Iggy found him under the pew," Bertha countered, her eyes probing. I nodded. "I doubt anyone would crawl under a pew without a good reason, even if he was, say, poisoned."

"Then you might be right. He could have had a spell put on him. That could explain his demise and his odd location. Do you have any idea what kind of spell might have been used?"

Pondering the question, Bertha's lips pressed together. "I'm not versed in every spell, so I can't say I know of one in particular that would do that. However, I do know that Hugo, for one, possesses the ability to manipulate a person into doing something against their will. There may be others with enough power to perform such a feat too."

I hoped she wasn't suggesting that Iggy's best friend was guilty of murder. Besides, he was a gargoyle shifter who rarely left the Hex and Bones back room. "Any specific names come to mind?"

A small smile tugged at the corners of Bertha's mouth. "How about you find out how he died first, and then come back to me? I'll see if I can gather a few names for you."

"You're the best. Is Genevieve around by any chance?"

"No, she and Hugo are out and about."

Hugo usually only went out when he was in her presence since she provided some kind of energy source for him. It wasn't something I truly understood.

"Do you think Genevieve might know who would want to harm Mr. Hastings?" I asked.

Bertha glanced off to the side. "She might have some insights, but I believe the sheriff would have a better chance of uncovering information from Harold's house. The problem is that the man was a hoarder. I'm not sure if anyone would find anything of value there."

That implied she'd been there. Hmm.

"What about his shop? Is there a chance something of significance could be found there?" Jaxson chimed in.

Bertha shrugged. "I couldn't say. I wish I could be of more help."

"You were of great help," I replied sincerely.

"Oh, and congratulations—or rather, future congratulations," Bertha said with a warm smile.

"Thank you."

As we exited the shop, Jaxson drew closer to me. "I suppose you want to check with the sheriff now, even though he probably doesn't know any more than we do about Harold's death. Not only that, we can't convince him Harold was murdered."

I grinned. "That may be, but I'd still like to see what he knows."

"To the sheriff's office we go then," he replied playfully.

Our destination was a mere one block down the street. Jennifer Lawson was manning the front desk since Pearl—an excellent gossip source—was attending our wedding reception.

"Hey, Jennifer," I greeted her casually.

"What are you two doing here? Shouldn't you be on your honeymoon, or are you waiting until the marriage is official?"

News traveled fast in Witch's Cove. "We plan to go somewhere at the end of the month. Is Steve in?"

"He just walked in, but I doubt he'll tell you much," Jennifer warned.

"That's okay. I have some information for him," I assured her. That was true, although I also said that to convince Jennifer to let us proceed. She was rather adamant about following protocol.

"Go on back," she said, finally relenting.

Jaxson and I entered Steve's office and found him standing behind his desk, engrossed in reading some papers.

He looked up and sighed. "Really? You two need to go."

I leaned against the desk and gave him my best look of

disappointment. "That's not nice. We're here to help. Don't forget all of the cases we've helped you solve in the past."

The sheriff's department often benefitted from our assistance since Witch's Cove teemed with people of magic.

"I am well aware of that, but... never mind. Have a seat."

Jaxson and I settled into the chairs. "For starters, we want to inform you that Harold was a warlock."

CHAPTER 4

"Harold Hastings was a warlock? Are you sure? Who is your reference? Or can you just tell?" the sheriff inquired.

"I personally haven't spent enough time around him to know for sure, but Iggy told me that Hugo had mentioned it. Since Hugo is unable to speak and serve as a witness, we have Bertha Murdoch, Aunt Fern, and none other than Gertrude Poole who can attest to Harold's magical abilities," I explained.

The sheriff let out a sigh, reaching for a trusty yellow pad of paper from his drawer. Despite my suggestion of going digital, he insisted on sticking to the old-fashioned method of pen and paper, claiming it was safer. It might be safer unless someone managed to steal the pad.

"How would Harold Hastings' magical talents have influenced his death?" the sheriff inquired.

I glanced over at Jaxson for him to explain.

"Bertha and Glinda think he could have fallen victim to a spell. If that turns out to be the case, you may require our—specifically Glinda's—assistance."

I was about to emphasize that we worked together as a team, but I knew Steve understood Jaxson's point. Our sheriff was quick on the uptake.

Without missing a beat, Steve raised an eyebrow. "You've had an hour or two to figure this out. Who do you suspect put a spell on Harold?"

Although sarcasm wasn't his usual style, no law enforcement officer appreciated being told how to do their job. I took a deep breath before responding, "We don't have any suspects yet." I raised a finger. "However, I must mention Priscilla Primm."

"The thirty-four-year-old who believes she'll soon be touring the country for her books?" Steve inquired, jotting down her name on his pad.

"Yes, that's the one. Aunt Fern brought her up as a possibility." I elaborated on my aunt's reasoning.

Steve struggled to contain his amusement. "Let me get this straight. A young woman wanted to purchase a valuable book at Harold's antique store. When Harold refused or couldn't sell it to her, she decided to kill him. Is Priscilla a witch too?"

"No!" I exclaimed, eager to clarify.

"I'm a bit confused. I thought you and Bertha theorized that someone with magical abilities might have cast a spell on Harold, which then caused his death?"

He was putting words in my mouth. The pressure of not having married the man I loved because of a mishap must have been affecting my clear thinking. "I'm not making any definitive statements. It's possible that Priscilla managed to steal the book, learn a spell, and cast it upon Harold."

"Interesting. I thought only witches and warlocks could perform spells, and yet you're claiming she isn't one," Steve mused, jotting down notes that appeared more like scribbles than words to me.

I shook my head. "I consider the chances of Priscilla being the murderer rather low."

Steve raised an eyebrow. "Oh, so now you're saying that Harold was murdered? You do realize he was nearly seventy. While not ancient, people do pass away from natural causes at that age."

Jaxson reached out, placing a comforting hand over mine. "Steve, all we're suggesting is that magic may have been involved. If you require our assistance, you know where to find us."

"Thank you, Jaxson. That's very generous of you both."

"One more question. Who was Harold's next of kin?" I asked.

"I would say you need to let me handle the details, but I'm sure with Jaxson's excellent computer skills, he'll find out soon enough, so I'll save him a few minutes of his time." Steve checked his pad. "Harold and his wife were divorced years ago, but they have a son who lives in the Florida Panhandle. From what I've gathered, he's an upstanding citizen."

That meant he had no arrests. To be honest, I'd met many people who were *upstanding citizens* and yet were killers. "Thank you."

Steve flipped over his yellow pad. "Enjoy the rest of your day. I'm hoping my grandmother saved a slice of your wedding cake for me."

I inwardly chastised myself for not thinking to grab some cake for Steve and Nash. "I hope she did too."

I stood, and Jaxson followed suit. As we exited the office, I let out a sigh. "That was unproductive. I should have asked if Steve intends to search Harold's shop for clues."

Jaxson spun me around, pulling me into a tight embrace, and whispered in my ear, "How about we let Steve handle the case for a while? I'm confident he'll thoroughly investigate everything. If he needs our help, he won't hesitate to ask."

Jaxson was right. I had a tendency to become overly obsessed with things. Leaning back, I relaxed. "Then how about we make some popcorn and watch a movie?"

He gave me a playful wink. "And afterward?"

I smiled mischievously. "We'll see!"

Upon entering through the side entrance of the Tiki Hut Restaurant to head upstairs, I spotted Iggy perched on the checkout counter. "Let me grab my little lizard, and I'll meet you upstairs," I told Jaxson.

"Perfect. It sounds as if the festivities have come to an end anyway. By the way, my parents are spending the night at the hotel, so I'd like to have a chat with them tomorrow before they head back home," Jaxson informed me.

"Of course," I replied.

"What movie do you want to watch?" he asked.

"Pick out any one you want."

"Any movie?" he asked, a glint of excitement in his eyes.

I had been preoccupied since Harold's death and hadn't paid enough attention to him. I wanted to make it up to him. "Any movie you want, Jaxson."

He hurried upstairs while I went to get Iggy. "Ready to go upstairs, little buddy?"

"Yes, but I think I'll visit with Aimee. I don't want to see you two make out."

We had talked about what it would be like once Jaxson moved in. I'd promised him nothing would change, but Iggy didn't seem to believe me. "I think that's a great idea."

Aimee was Aunt Fern's cat. While Aimee could talk due to a strange spell that literally fell on her, she wasn't technically my aunt's familiar either.

I carried Iggy upstairs. When I set him down, he hopped in through the cat door on Aunt Fern's side of the hall, and I went into my apartment. As soon as I stepped in, I could smell and hear the popcorn popping.

I walked into our tiny kitchen. "You move quickly."

"I like popcorn. What can I say?"

I FELT A NUDGE FROM JAXSON. "Glinda, your phone is ringing."

Rubbing my eyes, I sat up in bed where he handed me the phone. It was morning. "Who is it?"

I could have checked the caller ID myself, but my vision had yet to fully focus.

"Elissa."

My heart skipped a beat. Was she calling about Harold Hastings' autopsy? Elissa rarely contacted me unless she required my assistance. "Hello, Elissa."

"Glinda, I hate to bother you, but could you stop by the morgue and bring your necklace with you?"

I mentally pumped my fist. "Absolutely. Let me throw on some clothes and down a cup of coffee. Then I'll head on over."

"Great. Thank you."

I hung up and couldn't help but smile.

"It seems our esteemed medical examiner is stumped," Jaxson commented. "That might indicate that magic played a role in Harold's death."

"I'm hoping so." Filled with excitement, I sprung out of bed and opened the bottom drawer of my dresser where I kept clothes specifically reserved for visits to the morgue. It was often challenging to rid them of the lingering scent of death, so I kept them separate from my other clothes.

"While you work your magic, I'll swing by the hotel and spend some time with my parents," Jaxson said.

"Maybe we can have lunch together or something when I'm done and have cleaned up." I enjoyed spending time with them.

"I'll mention it, but they might be planning to head home. We did chat at the reception last night."

"I know. Tell them we promise we'll visit soon."

Jaxson leaned over and planted a kiss on my lips. "Will do. Text me when you're back."

"Okay."

I swiftly changed into my grubby clothes. No sooner had I pulled on my pants than Iggy waddled into the room. "Uh-oh. You're going to the morgue, aren't you?"

"You can smell something?" I found that slightly unnerving as I had washed the clothes.

"No, I heard you talking. I have excellent hearing, remember?"

"All too well."

Iggy turned around. "Where are you off to, mister?"

"To visit Aunt Fern. At least she'll give me some lettuce leaves to munch on." With that, Iggy scurried into the living room. The swinging cat door confirmed his departure.

Needing my morning caffeine rush, I hurried into the kitchen and reheated the leftover coffee from last night. Jaxson and I had enjoyed two movies, which explained why I had slept in. I added an extra scoop of sugar and then gulped down the less-than-perfect-tasting drink, but it would have to suffice.

Normally, I walked to the morgue, but Elissa seemed stressed, so I decided to drive instead. Once I parked, I hurried inside to find her waiting for me. Usually, she was in the autopsy room. Something peculiar seemed to be afoot.

"Good, you're here," Elissa greeted me. "I contacted you because, honestly, I can't find a single explanation for Harold's death."

"He was a warlock, so perhaps a disgruntled acquaintance decided to eliminate him."

"Steve called and informed me of your theory. Can you work your magic on him to see if I missed something?"

"I can. If witchcraft is involved, the stone will turn yellow." Both Elissa and I understood the significance of each color.

"Please come inside," Elissa beckoned.

As I entered the chilly room, poor Mr. Hastings lay on the table, thankfully concealed beneath a sheet. There was no need for his skin to be exposed for me to perform my investigation.

From routine, I removed my necklace and held it over his feet. Swinging it slowly, I gradually made my way up his body, closely observing any changes in the stone's color. Given his age, I anticipated the stone would turn green as it passed his heart area, indicating a potential blockage, which would imply a heart attack. However, when I reached that area, the stone didn't turn green; instead, it transformed into yellow.

"Witchcraft," the medical examiner proclaimed.

"Apparently so, but allow me to proceed." It would be rare for the stone to change colors mid-examination, but there was always a first time for everything. If it did, it might imply, say, he had been poisoned before a spell was cast upon him.

I swear I wasn't anticipating what occurred next, but as I passed the stone over his throat, it took on a purple hue. Although Elissa probably wanted to inquire about it, she understood that I needed to conclude the examination. The strangest part was that as the stone moved over his face, the purple shade became more prominent. "That is odd," I commented.

"I agree. If purple indicates poison, why didn't anything

change when you passed the stone over his abdomen?" Elissa questioned.

"I believe it might have been a magical kind of poison that doesn't come in a liquid form."

"You mean he didn't ingest it?"

"That would be my guess."

"A spell caused his demise?" she asked.

I couldn't blame Elissa for sounding skeptical. After all, she wasn't a witch. The fact that she trusted my necklace spoke volumes about her open-mindedness. Besides, she was the doctor, and I was just a former teacher turned waitress turned amateur sleuth. However, I was a witch. "That would be my guess," I replied.

"Is this the kind of spell you could have performed?" Elissa inquired.

I turned to face her. "No. First of all, I don't dabble in dark magic. That's a different realm altogether."

"Oh, I didn't mean to offend."

I raised my hand reassuringly. "No offense taken. I just need another cup of coffee, that's all."

Elissa exhaled audibly. "Steve won't be pleased when I include 'cause of death unknown' in the autopsy report."

"No, he won't." I glanced at Harold's lifeless form but didn't notice any visible bruising on his forehead. "Were there any external injuries? Perhaps someone tried to restrain him, but he managed to break free."

"He did have some bruises here and there, but that's not uncommon for a man of his age. He wasn't in the best physical condition. I will run more toxicology screens for poisons, but you might have to do some investigating on this one."

"Seems so." The problem was that I had no idea where to begin.

CHAPTER 5

When I returned to the apartment, I had to shower in order to wash away any lingering scent of the morgue. The odor of death had a way of sticking to every pore, leaving an unpleasant residue.

After quickly cleaning up, I changed into fresh clothes just as Jaxson walked in. "You're back! Did your parents leave?" I asked, eager for an update.

"They did. Mom had something to take care of, but she sent her love," Jaxson replied with a warm smile.

I couldn't help but return the smile. "I really like your mother."

Jaxson pulled me into a hug. "I've been thinking."

I leaned back, curiosity piqued. "Always dangerous."

He playfully tapped my nose and stepped back. "If we want to learn more about Harold and any potential warlock enemies, what do you think about taking a trip to the Panhandle to visit his son?"

"Really? That's a fantastic idea. I don't recall the sheriff telling us the exact location or his son's name."

Jaxson chuckled. "Oh, ye of little faith. That's what computers are for."

"Good thinking. I know Iggy will want to come along. He's with Aimee right now. Let me grab him."

"How about we both pack an overnight bag? While you finish up—since it will take you longer—I'll head over to the office to find the son's address. Grab Iggy and meet me there, okay?" Jaxson asked.

I stood on my tiptoes to give him a kiss. "Will do."

Once Jaxson finished stuffing a change of clothes and some toiletries into his bag, he left. I then finished packing and made my way across the hall to Aunt Fern's apartment. Using the key she had given me, I let myself in.

"Iggy?"

My familiar waddled over, his eyes curious. "You called?"

I explained our plan to drive to the Panhandle. While we could potentially make it a day trip, it seemed wiser to stay overnight considering the uncertainty of the visit. "Do you want to come with us or stay here?"

"I want to come. You might need my cloaking abilities," Iggy replied confidently.

Iggy's skill of remaining unseen had proven valuable on previous occasions. "I'm not certain if this will be that kind of trip, but I can't rule it out."

He looked at me eagerly. "Where's Jaxson?"

"He's at the office," I replied, lifting Iggy into my arms. "Come on, let's go see if he found any information about our destination."

The office was just a short distance away, and we quickly arrived. Climbing the stairs, I stepped inside and greeted Jaxson. "Hi."

He turned around, a hint of excitement in his eyes. "I think I found what we need."

"That was fast." Jaxson always impressed me with his speed.

Jaxson winked. "I'm just that good. The son's name is Charles Hastings. He's married with two young kids. It's about a four-hour drive to reach their place, so we should get on the road."

"Road trip!" Iggy exclaimed, his enthusiasm infectious. "Make sure to pack plenty of lettuce for me."

"Don't worry, I won't forget," I assured him.

Jaxson packed up his computer, ready to embark on our journey.

"THIS IS IT. The yellow house with the black shutters," I remarked, double-checking the GPS on my phone to confirm our arrival.

Jaxson glanced at the car parked in the driveway. "The car implies he might be home." He turned off the engine.

I almost mentioned that the car might belong to Charles' wife, but Jaxson had already discovered she worked outside the home.

As Jaxson made his way to my side, I carefully placed Iggy inside my large bag. "Please stay put, Iggy. We don't want you wandering around."

"What if I cloak myself?" Iggy suggested.

I shook my head firmly. "There's no reason to suspect Charles of any wrongdoing. Okay?"

Iggy reluctantly slid down into my purse, his disagreement evident. Jaxson opened my car door, and we proceeded to the front of the house. He knocked, and a man in his early forties answered.

"Yes?" the man inquired.

"Mr. Hastings?" Jaxson asked politely.

"Yes," Charles replied.

"We're from Witch's Cove. We're sorry about your dad."

""Thank you, but Dad and I weren't close, at least not in recent years," Charles shared.

Surprisingly, I didn't sense a whole lot of pain coming from the man, but everyone grieved differently. I'd love to dig into that issue. I also wanted to know why he didn't rush to Witch's Cove to see about the funeral arrangements, but I didn't want to alienate him right off the bat.

"We were hoping you could answer a few questions for us," Jaxson explained.

A hint of tension creased Charles' jawline. "You reporters?"

Iggy chose that moment to poke his head out of my bag. "No, we're investigators. We want to find out who killed your dad."

Charles froze, whether from shock at the sight of a pink iguana or from the realization that we were interested in his father's case, I couldn't tell. Although his father was a warlock, it didn't necessarily mean Charles possessed the same abilities. I'd come across a few exceptions.

He shifted his gaze to Jaxson. "You a warlock too?"

"No, sir," Jaxson replied.

"But I'm a witch, and this here is Iggy." The only way he'd assume that would be if he understood my cute iguana. "We truly want to help. May we come in? I have an idea of what happened to your dad, but I need more information," I explained, hoping to convey our sincerity.

Charles hesitated for a moment before stepping aside.

"Sure, but my wife and kids are due home shortly. We don't discuss witchcraft in this house."

"I understand," I replied, although I couldn't fully comprehend it. After all, I was born and raised in Witch's Cove, a place where witches of all kinds were accepted and embraced—usually. Our discussion of what caused the rift between him and his father might have to wait. I didn't get the vibe that he'd killed his dad, but I'd been wrong about people before.

The interior of Charles' home exuded an upscale atmosphere, blending contemporary and modern elements. It was a departure from what I would have expected considering his father's penchant for antiques.

"Please, have a seat. Can I offer you something to drink?" Charles asked.

"No, thank you. We're good," Jaxson told him as we both settled onto the sofa.

We didn't want to waste any time, so I briefly explained how we became aware of his father's death.

"Let me start by saying that I have a particular talent for determining the possible cause of death. When the medical examiner couldn't find any evidence to explain your father's passing, she reached out to me. I concluded that magic was the cause."

Charles ran a hand through his hair, displaying frustration. "Wouldn't you know it?"

Jaxson leaned forward. "Wouldn't we know what?"

Charles took a moment before responding. "Let me give you a brief history of my dad. Being known as a person of magic in this town is highly disapproved of. In fact, when people found out about his abilities, they practically chased him out of town."

"Did he use his magic to harm someone?" I inquired, searching for an explanation.

"In a way. An acquaintance, who had limited warlock powers, was having trouble with some deer destroying his vegetable garden. Joseph sought my dad's help since he was known for his immense power. Dad cast a containment spell around Joseph's plants to deter the deer. It worked for a day, but the next day, five dead deer were found next to the plants. Joseph only wanted the deer to stay away—not die."

I gasped. "Did Joseph think your dad caused their death?"

"I'm not sure, but animal control accused Joseph of killing the animals—which was illegal that time of year. He was even taken into custody."

"But the animals didn't have any wounds, right?" I asked, trying to piece the puzzle together.

"No, they didn't. So they let Joseph go. Unfortunately, Joseph revealed to the police what had truly happened and that my dad was responsible. While it was true that my father made the spell, Joseph's reputation suffered immensely, and he was essentially driven out of town too."

My mind raced with possibilities. "Do you think Joseph could have been the one who put a spell on your dad as a form of revenge?"

Charles pondered for a moment. "I wouldn't rule him out."

Jaxson chimed in, "Where is Joseph now?"

"I have no idea."

"What's his last name?" Jaxson asked.

"Andrews."

Curiosity must have gotten the bests of Iggy, because he popped his head out of my bag. "When did your dad leave town?"

"Right after that incident with Joseph. It's why my father chose Witch's Cove though he claimed he was going to live his life as an ordinary human. I can't say if he succeeded or not."

Although I didn't often utilize magic, I knew that when I did, it had its risks. It was hard to fathom that Harold would completely abandon his magical abilities upon arriving in our town, however. "I understand. Spells can go wrong."

Iggy poked his head out of my bag again. "You can say that again. Glinda did a spell to turn me back to green and ended up seeing ghosts."

"Hush, Iggy," I whispered.

"The bottom line for me was that I felt as if my dad disowned his family. He wasn't here for my wedding. No dad should be like that." Charles stood. "But if you think I might know something, please feel free to reach out to me." He located a business card from the coffee table drawer and handed it to us. It had his phone number and email address on it.

I didn't comment that he could have visited his dad since Witch's Cove wasn't that far away, but to miss his son's wedding wasn't good. I assumed Harold had been out of town at the time. There had to be more to the story, but I didn't want to push Charles to share if he wasn't comfortable with doing so. We could always come back if need be.

"One final question. Is there anyone else who might know more about your dad's abilities? Or who his enemies might have been," I asked.

Chances were Harold upset others before he was run out of town.

Charles averted his gaze momentarily. "I would suggest reaching out to Gus Littlefield. I believe my dad and Gus kept in touch after Dad left. Let me fetch his contact information." He disappeared into another room. When he returned, he handed us a piece of paper. "Here."

"Thank you." I expressed our gratitude for his willingness to talk with us.

Making sure Iggy was secure in my purse, we left his house, ready to pursue the next lead.

Once we were both in the car, I took out my phone and quickly entered the new address. "It's only about five miles from here. Go to the end of the road and take a right," I instructed.

Jaxson followed my directions, and as we drove, he broke the silence. "What do you make of the dad's reason for leaving town?"

"Charles' reasoning makes sense to me," I replied. "Not everyone is a fan of witchcraft."

Jaxson seemed to think about that. "And Charles? Could he have wanted to get back at his father for abandoning his family?"

"I suppose it's possible, but he's not high on my list as the murderer. Witchcraft wasn't a topic he seemed interested in discussing."

Jaxson nodded. For the remainder of the short trip, our conversation was limited to me giving him directions. I had a feeling that Jaxson needed some time to process everything that had happened—as did I. Even Iggy, my usually talkative familiar, remained unusually quiet.

"There's Gus' place," I pointed out. The duplex appeared rundown, but the yard was surprisingly well-maintained. There was no car in the driveway, but that didn't necessarily mean he wasn't home.

We both stepped out of the car and headed toward the front door. I rang the bell, and a moment later Iggy looked up at me. "I hear someone."

Sure enough, after a few seconds, an elderly gentleman answered the door. "May I help you?" he asked politely.

I introduced Jaxson and myself. "We're from Witch's Cove," I began.

The man's eyes lit up. "Did Harold send you?"

"I wish he had," I replied. "Actually, his son gave us your address."

The man's expression fell, his chest deflating. "Is Harold...dead or something?"

"I'm afraid Harold was murdered yesterday," I informed him, bracing myself for his reaction.

The news hit him hard, and if Jaxson hadn't stepped around me and grabbed the man's arm, he might have stumbled backward. "Why don't you sit down, sir," Jaxson gently coaxed as he led him to the nearby sofa.

"Can I get you some water?" I asked.

"Not yet. Please sit, and tell me everything," Gus managed to say, his voice filled with a mixture of shock and grief.

I resumed my explanation, recounting the events that led us to Gus' doorstep. I mentioned how Iggy, our ring bearer, had spotted the body and accidentally swallowed the ring. Iggy, of course, couldn't resist making his presence known and introducing himself.

"He's a cute fellow, isn't he?" Gus commented, a faint smile breaking through his sorrow.

"I think so," I replied. "Now, do you have any idea who might have wanted Harold dead?"

CHAPTER 6

"No, I don't. Sure, Harold had his enemies. Don't we all? But would someone really go as far as to kill him?" Gus shook his head, seemingly unsure.

Jaxson chimed in. "Sometimes, the person who dislikes someone might not show it openly."

Gus snapped his fingers as if a realization had struck him. "Alistair Brooklyn. He's the one. It must be him."

Now, I was intrigued. "And why do you think that?"

"About a year before Harold moved to Witch's Cove, he felt that Alistair was using his magic for nefarious purposes, though Harold never gave me the details."

"Are you saying that Mr. Brooklyn practiced dark magic?" I hadn't expected that revelation.

"Yes," Gus confirmed. "Let me explain. You need to understand that Harold was a powerful warlock, although his powers seemed to have diminished lately due to a lack of practice."

At that moment, Iggy popped his head up. "I'm not following," he piped up.

Gus chuckled and addressed my familiar. "Apologies,

young man. Not being a fan of the use of dark magic, Harold cast a spell on Alistair to weaken his evil powers. I think Harold felt bad about having to do that and decided to curtail his own use of magic."

"Ouch," Iggy replied sympathetically.

"Exactly," Gus nodded. "When Alistair discovered what had been done to him, he was furious. Granted, he wasn't able to do much at the time since his powers had been dampened, but if he did end up killing Harold, his strength must have returned."

That motive for murder seemed plausible, though if Alistair's powers had returned, why kill Harold? Revenge maybe? "Does Alistair still live here in town?"

Gus shook his head. "No, he's much more cunning than that. I heard he followed Harold and moved to a nearby town about a year later. He might have waited that long in the hopes his powers would return. If they did or didn't, I couldn't say since I didn't speak with him much."

"Do you remember the name of this nearby town?"

Gus looked up, deep in thought. "Not exactly. I think it had the word 'palm' in its name."

"Palm Ridge?" It was a town very close to Witch's Cove.

Gus raised his finger in confirmation. "Yes, that's the one."

Jaxson leaned forward, his elbows on his knees. "Were you in contact with Harold after he left?"

Gus nodded. "Yes, although not as frequently of late. We used to video conference when we wanted to chat."

While this information held potential, our best chance of finding the killer lay in uncovering the details of Harold's death. If Alistair's powers had weakened significantly, it would cast doubt on his ability to perform a powerful spell—unless his powers had returned.

"Are you familiar with any spells that could kill someone?" I inquired, hoping for some insight.

Gus' eyes widened in alarm. "I don't dabble in dark magic. Never have."

"Me neither," I quickly assured him.

"Besides Alistair, are there any other individuals who might have wanted Harold dead?" Jaxson asked.

Gus had said no before, but maybe a name had occurred to him.

He glanced to the side, appearing lost in thought, and then shook his head. "Not that I know of, but if you leave your contact information, I'll ask around discreetly and let you know if I learn anything."

"Thank you. Is there anyone else we should speak to?" I asked, hoping for more leads.

"Harold mostly kept to himself," Gus replied with a hint of resignation.

Realizing there were no further immediate leads to pursue, we exchanged contact information with Gus. Once we hopped in the car, Jaxson looked over at me. "It's getting late. How about we grab something to eat and find a place to spend the night?"

"Sounds good to me."

Iggy poked his head out of my bag. "What about me?"

His statement confused me. "What about you?"

"I don't want to be in the same room as you two if... You know...things get romantic," Iggy explained.

His remark brought a smile to my face. "We'll make sure to keep our kissing very quiet."

Iggy seemed unsure. "I might have to sleep in the lobby."

"We'll see."

On our way back to town, we stumbled upon a charming restaurant. Considering Iggy's mood, I asked if he wanted to join us in the restaurant where he'd have to stay hidden, or if he wanted to remain in the car where the temperature would still be comfortable for him.

"I'll come with you, but make sure to ask for some lettuce," Iggy replied.

I chuckled. "As if I wouldn't." I snapped my purse closed to ensure no one caught sight of him. I didn't want to cause a commotion, which I knew about all too well.

Once inside the restaurant, we were led to a secluded booth in the back, providing us with some privacy. After ordering our drinks, I glanced around to make sure no one could overhear our conversation. Talking about magic—and murder—in a town not used to such stuff, wouldn't go over well.

"What are your thoughts about who did it?" I asked.

"How about you list the potential suspects and their motives, and I'll let you know if I agree or not," Jaxson suggested.

Compiling the list was challenging. "First is Priscilla Primm, the aspiring author with no magical abilities. She desperately wants to be a famous author and thought what Harold had was her ticket to success. Next is the son, Charles Hastings. Due to his resentment toward his father's lack of attention, he might have killed his dad, but that would only ensure that the family was never together."

"I'll agree with you on both of those points," Jaxson shot back.

"Then there is Joseph Andrews, the man troubled by the deer. I suppose if I was accused of murdering animals, brought in for questioning because of Harold's mishandling of magic, and then run out of town, I might want to do him in too."

"That's reasonable, but I doubt the man is powerful enough. If he had been, he could have put a spell on his vegetable garden and kept the animals out himself."

"Good point."

"Next?" Jaxson asked.

"Alistair Brooklyn. Even though his diminished magic should eliminate him as a suspect, we don't know if his magic has returned or not."

"Is that even possible?" he asked.

"I honestly don't know."

"So, we have Priscilla, Charles, Joseph, and Alistair. Who are you leaning toward?" Jaxson asked.

"That's a tough one. I hope we have more options since their motives seem weak. If I had to pick one, I'd choose Joseph, despite him possibly not having enough powers. He could have hired someone to put a spell on Harold."

"That makes sense. Is it possible that Priscilla also hired someone to steal the item she desired, and Harold caught this person in the act? Fearing the consequences, the thief could have resorted to using a deadly spell on Harold. An elderly man might succumb to such magic," Jaxson said.

Doubt crept in, and I sighed. "We need Levy."

"What do you think he can do?"

"He and his coven possess almost every spell book that ever existed. Somewhere in that extensive library of his, we might find a spell that our killer employed," I explained.

"We should also ask if a person's magic has been weakened, whether it can be restored," Jaxson threw in.

"Excellent point."

The waitress arrived with our drinks, breaking our conversation. "Have you decided what you'd like to order?" she asked.

I smiled politely. "Not just yet." I sensed Iggy squirming in my purse. As soon as the waitress departed, I opened it slightly. "I haven't forgotten about you."

"You better not have," Iggy warned.

I refocused on Jaxson. "Honestly, I'm hoping that if dark magic was indeed used against Harold then someone from Levy's coven might be able to provide crucial information."

"If dark magic is involved, it wouldn't be wise to get too close to this person if we learn who it is," Jaxson cautioned.

That was the challenge we faced. "I know. We'll have to find a way to lure them into revealing themselves."

Jaxson took a sip of his beer. "You do realize that we're entering extremely dangerous territory, right? Your magic is remarkable, but if we're dealing with dark magic, can you counter it?"

It was a rhetorical question. "No, but who says I have to be the one to confront this individual?"

"We both know the sheriff won't be able to do much," Jaxson acknowledged.

A smile crossed my face. "Yes, but do we know someone who isn't affected by spells?"

Iggy popped his head up excitedly. "Me?"

I was surprised by his suggestion. "No, not you, though I appreciate the offer. I was thinking of your best friend."

"Hugo!" Iggy exclaimed, catching onto my idea.

Looking at Jaxson, I nodded. "Hugo, and perhaps Genevieve. As gargoyles, they won't be affected by dark magic like humans are—or so I hope. I'm not saying we'll have to resort to using them, but I'm keeping an open mind."

"I like the way you think," Jaxson agreed.

UPON OUR RETURN to Witch's Cove around noon the next day, a note awaited us on our apartment door. I peeled it off and unfolded it. "It's from Steve. He wants to see us."

Jaxson unlocked the door. "I'm guessing that he received the autopsy report, which would state that the cause of death is unknown. Elissa probably slipped him a note mentioning your use of the necklace and the possibility of magic being involved."

"That's probably the case," I replied, stepping into the apartment and setting down my belongings.

Iggy hopped out of my purse. "Phew. I'm glad to be back."

"Me, too, but since Jaxson and I are just going to rehash what we learned to the sheriff, you might want to chat with Aunt Fern instead of sitting through a boring meeting."

"Good idea. I'll go down and tell her about our trip," Iggy said. "Besides, she'll give me food."

"She will at that," I replied.

Once Iggy slipped through the cat door—or rather the iguana door—I turned to Jaxson. "Let me change, and then we can see what Steve wants to tell us."

"I'll join you," Jaxson agreed.

I kept forgetting that we were now an almost-married couple. After freshening up, we made our way over to the sheriff's office. Inside, Steve's grandmother was manning the reception desk.

"Pearl, how are you?" I greeted her.

She put away her knitting. "Me? I'm great. Did you two take a quick quasi-honeymoon yesterday?"

I wondered if they were keeping tabs on us now or if Aunt Fern had mentioned something to her good friend. I chuckled, deciding to play along. "We haven't officially tied the knot, so no official honeymoon. No, we went to speak with Harold Hastings' son."

Pearl's expression turned solemn. "Oh, the poor man. How is he taking his father's death?"

I wondered if she knew something. "He's sad, but they weren't particularly close."

Pearl nodded, seemingly aware of the situation. "Harold mentioned something to that fact. I used to visit his shop now and then. He had so many treasures in that store. Do you have any idea who might have killed him?"

We had a case to solve, and we probably shouldn't be spending too much time on gossip that would spread in town like wildfire. "Not yet." I waved the note Steve had written. "The sheriff asked us to stop by."

"Of course. He and Nash are in his office. Go on back," Pearl directed us.

"Thanks," I replied. As we entered Steve's office, Nash stood and pulled over an extra chair. Steve nodded and then raised his eyebrows. "You've been gone."

Feeling a bit self-conscious, I wondered if everyone had noticed our absence. "We thought we'd take a road trip to the Panhandle."

Steve's tone turned serious. "Don't tell me you interrogated Harold's son?"

Not fond of the negative connotation associated with the word *interrogated,* I glanced at Jaxson for help. Accusations always bothered me when they were unjustified.

Jaxson stepped in, hopefully to clarify. "Steve, we simply wanted to see if the son could provide us with a clue as to who might have wanted to harm his father. That's all."

The sheriff picked up his yellow pad, indicating his readiness to listen. "Tell me what you learned."

Between the two of us, we filled him in on our observations regarding the son, his possible suggestion for a suspect, and our discussion with Harold's friend, Gus.

"You two have been busy," Steve remarked.

I was curious to know what progress he and Nash had made. "And you?"

Steve flipped through some pages. "I don't have much, but according to our esteemed and gossipy diner owner, Esmeralda Evergreen, aka Katie Altman, has been upset with Harold for weeks. He came into possession of a rare mystical plant book, and she told him she was planning to buy it as soon as she withdrew the money from the bank."

"Don't tell me, he sold it to someone else instead?" I asked.

"You guessed it. Esmeralda wasn't happy. Do you know if she is a witch or not?" Steve inquired.

"She is, but I've never discussed her specific talents with her. Given her incredible plant-growing abilities, I always suspected she used magic to produce such amazing blooms," I explained.

Jaxson looked over at me and then at Nash and Steve. "We should probably speak with the Oglethorpes. Don't they often get flowers for their shop from Esmeralda's nursery? She might have shared some gossip about Harold with them."

"That's an excellent idea," I said.

"Normally, it would be my job to interview them, but since they are friends of your family and you can speak their magical language, it makes more sense for you to handle it," Steve said.

I found his term *magical language* endearing. "Will do. Are there any other potential suspects?"

"No, but we found a pencil in Harold's hand. It appears he was trying to write something, but all we could make out was a line," Steve shared.

"It looked more like a scuff mark to me," Nash added.

"Too bad. I guess that would have been too easy if he wrote the name of his killer on the wooden floor," I commented. "Do you have any idea how he ended up under the pew? It couldn't have been an easy feat for an older man."

"I'm sure we'll find out with time," Steve responded.

Jaxson placed a hand on my arm, a signal that it was time for us to leave. We had plenty of work to do.

CHAPTER 7

Since we had only consumed coffee for breakfast and then driven to Witch's Cove, hunger began to gnaw at me. "I would suggest stopping at the diner for a good brunch, but I'm willing to bet Dolly has already informed Pearl or Steve about everything she knows."

Jaxson smiled. "Coffee or tea?"

I chuckled. "You know me well. I have no idea if Maude or Miriam will be the best source of gossip, but since we're already on this side of the street, how about the Bubbling Cauldron Coffee Shop?"

"Works for me," he agreed.

As we entered the coffee shop, Miriam glanced up and waved. Once she finished with a customer, she made her way over to us, promptly pulled out a chair, and sat down. I always loved it when she did that.

Miriam placed a comforting hand over mine. "How are you holding up? I can't imagine how disappointed you must be to have your wedding interrupted—all because of a dead body."

I acknowledged my disappointment but remained optimistic about our impending official marriage. "The most traumatic part was Iggy swallowing the ring."

Miriam seemed taken aback. "That part was real?"

It appeared that the town's gossip tree wasn't as accurate as I had thought. "Yes, it was, but Gertrude and I managed to use a little magic to retrieve it."

"Thank goodness," she replied.

Eager to discuss the investigation, I lowered my voice. "So, have you and the ladies come up with a list of potential suspects in Harold Hastings' murder?"

Miriam leaned closer, her voice hushed. "I know your aunt mentioned Priscilla Primm. She has potential, but personally, I'd point my finger at Edgar Eccleston."

I wracked my brain, struggling to recall the name. "Who is he?"

"I suppose you're too young to know him. Not only that, you majored in math. Edgar is a professor of ancient history at Palm Ridge Junior College," Miriam informed us.

Understanding dawned on me. An ancient history professor might be interested in antiques. Maybe he had a run-in with Harold. "Why do you suspect him?"

"Maude was at the antique store the other day when Edgar came in. He was asking about The Enigma Stone book."

Jaxson's brows furrowed. "What's The Enigma Stone book about?"

Miriam blew out a breath. "I'm not entirely sure, but Maude overheard them discussing something about its mystical powers and how it could unlock the secrets of the universe."

"That would be some book!" I said.

"Agreed, but apparently, Harold let it be known that this book was on display, but it was from his personal collection and not for sale." Miriam seemed pleased with her contribution.

"That's valuable information. Did your sister happen to know if this professor is a warlock or not?" I asked.

Miriam shook her head. "Not within our realm of knowledge."

"I get it. Thanks anyway." There were two people waiting at the counter. "I can see you're busy, but could I order a cup of coffee and a pastry?"

"You got it," Miriam confirmed, before turning her attention to Jaxson. "Plain coffee, no pastry, right?"

"Normally, yes, but don't you serve egg burritos?" Jaxson asked.

"In the morning, but don't worry, I'll whip one up for you myself," Miriam assured him with a smile before heading back to the counter.

I leaned back in my chair, exhaling deeply once she was out of earshot. "Out of all the cases we've dealt with, I don't recall another one being this complicated. How can one seemingly nice man have so many enemies?"

"I don't know. You'll need to get out your whiteboard and list the suspects and their motives. That usually helps us. Then we'll have to verify who is a witch or warlock and who isn't."

He was absolutely right. "The only issue is that a non-witch could have hired someone with dark magic abilities to do their dirty work."

"Let's not get ahead of ourselves. Once we go over the suspects, we'll have to decide who to look into first," Jaxson reminded me, his level-headed nature shining through. "Often that takes us in a different direction."

"You're right. I'm guessing that Steve has already checked out Harold's store, but I'm betting he wouldn't know what was truly important and what wasn't."

Jaxson raised an eyebrow. "And we do?"

"Not precisely, but if *The Enigma Stone* is still there, we might be able to cross the professor off the list," I said.

"If it's gone, we'll have to see if he has it in his possession. If it is, it might mean he killed Harold for it."

"And if the book Priscilla Primm wanted is still at the shop, she might not be guilty either," I added. "We'll have to ask her what book or item she was wanting."

I made a mental note to compile a list of items from Harold's antique store that people had been asking for. Just then, Miriam approached our table to deliver our meal with a friendly smile. "Here you go. Let me know if you want me to ask around about anyone." She smiled and then winked.

I adored our gossip queens and appreciated their invaluable assistance in uncovering clues. "I most certainly will," I replied.

I took a sip of the perfectly balanced coffee that Miriam had prepared for me, savoring the blend of sugar, cream, and cinnamon. "Delicious."

Jaxson took a bite of his egg burrito. "Mmm. This hits the spot."

"I'm glad." Miriam then returned to the counter.

"I think I should call Levy to see if he has any idea what kind of spell would cause someone to drop dead like that."

Jaxson nodded. "If Harold was hiding under the church pew, he might have been trying to escape from someone. It's possible that this person chased Harold into the church thinking that no one would see him or her perform this dark spell. Even though Harold hid, the spell got to him."

"That would explain a lot."

Jaxson took a large gulp of his coffee and then set the cup down. "We know very little about this curse or whatever it was that killed him. It could have been a spell that made Harold so paranoid that he believed seeking refuge in the church would keep him safe. When he crawled under the pew, perhaps the stress or fear triggered a fatal heart attack," Jaxson theorized.

I considered his perspective. "I like your train of thought, but Elissa would have mentioned heart failure if that were the case of death, and the stone in my necklace wouldn't have turned yellow."

Jaxson looked off to the side. "True. We really do need Levy's expertise. Do you want to take Iggy with us when we visit him, assuming he's available?"

"That's a great idea. Iggy loves spending time in the library, and if Camila is there, she'll shower him with attention."

After finishing our meal, we paid the bill and made our way across the street to our apartment. I smiled, loving the idea of it being *our* apartment now rather than solely *mine*. Once inside, I dialed Levy Poole, Gertrude's knowledgeable warlock grandson who possessed a wealth of information about spells.

"Glinda? Is that really you? I thought you were mad at me or something," Levy said in a jovial greeting.

I chuckled. "Never. It's been a while since we've had a tricky murder in Witch's Cove."

Levy's tone turned serious. "My grandmother told me about the canceled wedding and Iggy's issue. I'm sorry I couldn't make it. I was out of town delivering a talk on our coven laws."

"I bet they appreciated that."

"I hope so. I heard that one of Witch's Cove's elderly gentlemen died in the church. If you're calling, I'm guessing you suspect witchcraft was involved," Levy deduced.

"That's right." I explained my use of the magical necklace on the body that revealed the presence of a spell. "Do you think we could meet you at your library—assuming you're free? I'd love to see if we can find a spell that would be able to kill a warlock without leaving any outward signs."

"I'm always willing to help. In fact, things have been rather dull in Hampton River. I'll call around and see if we can get some assistance. When can you come over?" Levy asked.

"We can leave in a few minutes," I replied.

"Perfect," Levy acknowledged.

Jaxson placed a hand on my arm. "I'll get Iggy. If we leave him out of this, he'll be in a snit for a while."

"Very true."

While Jaxson gathered Iggy, I quickly jotted down the names of the possible suspects and their potential motives. This information might give Levy and the coven an idea of what we were searching for.

Once Jaxson and Iggy returned, we departed. Hampton River was two towns over, and it only took about twenty minutes or so to reach our destination. From the outside, no one would suspect that this building contained one of the most extensive collections of magical books in all of Florida.

Jaxson parked the car. "Did you ask Levy if it's okay for me to see the coven's inner sanctum library?" he inquired.

"No, but you're with me. He knows you won't say anything," I assured him.

"He lets me go in," Iggy proudly added.

"That's because you're special," Jaxson playfully retorted.

Oh boy, Iggy's ego was already inflated enough.

There must have been a camera somewhere mounted outside, because as we approached the door with no handle, as I referred to it, Levy pushed it open from the inside.

"Welcome," he greeted us, briefly glancing at Jaxson without saying anything about a non-magical person entering the sacred area.

Though I had walked down this dark corridor many

times, I could always sense the tangible presence of magic in the air. When we reached the inner sanctum, two other coven members, Dax and Camila, were there.

It was interesting that a sweet scent lingered in the air, like incense and herbs had been smoldering for some time. The faint aroma of flowers and citrus blended with a hint of spice, creating a unique aroma that evoked feelings of peace and comfort. I hadn't been aware Levy's coven did spells in the library, but they must have.

"Iggy!" Camila exclaimed, opening her arms. Jaxson set Iggy on the table, and he waddled over to her.

"Hi, Camila," Iggy greeted her cheerfully.

Camila would keep him entertained while we conducted our research.

I introduced Jaxson to the two other coven members.

"Thanks for letting me be here," Jaxson said. "Glinda has talked about this place a lot." He scanned the extensive bookshelves. "I can see why."

"Our pleasure," Camila said.

"Have a seat and give us the details," Levy instructed.

Jaxson and I proceeded to provide them with a detailed account of what had transpired.

"If I had to point a finger at one of your suspects, I'd consider either Alistair Brooklyn or Edgar Eccleston," Levy said.

"But Levy, how many witches or warlocks have you known who have fully recovered after having their powers diminished?" Dax interjected. "If we're talking about a spell that can kill someone, that person would have to be well-versed in dark magic." Dax turned to us. "I'm afraid we don't associate with those circles very often, so our suspect pool isn't large."

"I understand," I said.

"Dax is right," Levy agreed. "Not only that, those practitioners of dark magic who are from here probably wouldn't have known Harold." He lifted a finger. "However, it's possible the spell Harold put on Alistair wasn't meant to be permanent. Even if it was designed that way, there are some spells that can reverse it. It's just not easy."

"Good to know. What are your thoughts on Professor Edgar Eccleston?" I asked.

"Before we condemn the poor man, let's search the books for any malevolent spells," Levy proposed. "Were you able to determine if Harold's death was quick or if it happened over a longer period of time?"

I shrugged. "My magical amulet wouldn't be able to provide me with that information."

"We'll inquire around once we return to Witch's Cove," Jaxson suggested. "I'm sure we can figure out who his regular patrons were. They might have noticed whether his health had declined in the last few weeks."

"That would be helpful to know," Levy agreed.

"Then let's scour the books for that spell," I suggested.

Dax pushed back his chair, eager to contribute. "I have a few ideas." He swiftly retrieved about ten books. "Let's each take two of these and see what we can find."

CHAPTER 8

I took my couple of books and began to search through them, knowing that finding what we were looking for wouldn't be an easy task. The ancient books didn't always provide a clear explanation regarding the purpose of the spells, which struck me as odd. They mostly just listed the ingredients along with the spell itself.

As we delved into the texts, Jaxson looked up from his book, skepticism written on his face. "Does all of this spell stuff actually work?" he asked the group.

I scooted closer to him, intrigued by his inquiry. "Are you referring to something specific?"

His eyes scanned the page and then tapped the page. "Right here, it says that the spell describes a seemingly straightforward process—lighting some herbs, uttering a few words, and the result would be the death of the targeted person. I find it hard to believe it can be that simple."

Camila chuckled. "You are partially right. The true power of the witch comes from the intent and skill behind the spell. If someone inexperienced attempted it, nothing significant would likely happen. Even if I tried it, the result might be that the person felt unwell. However, a truly powerful witch or warlock, especially one with bad intentions, could potentially use such magic to a deadly end, especially against someone already vulnerable or aged."

"Wow. Got it." Jaxson turned to me. "So is Gertrude capable of such malevolence?" he whispered.

"Heard that," Levy said. "Even if my grandmother could perform the spell effectively, she never would entertain the idea of trying such a dark spell. However, Harold is dead, so someone might have used a spell like this. Let me make a copy of it, just in case we stumble upon suspicious ingredients in our suspect's possession, which would elevate them on our list of potential culprits."

Jaxson agreed, passing the book to Levy and picking up another to continue our search.

The room fell into a thoughtful silence as we sifted through the old tomes, each of us absorbed in the quest for clues.

After a while, Dax piped up, excitement evident in his voice. "Check this out. It's a rather intriguing spell that involves a cursed artifact. According to the text, whoever possesses the artifact will gradually weaken over time."

My mind raced with the implications. "Do you think this weakening could lead to death?"

Dax's finger traced along the words. "The outcome is uncertain, but death seems possible."

"Does it say how long this slow decline takes? Are we talking hours, days, or weeks?" Jaxson asked.

"The text didn't provide a specific timeframe, as it depends on the sorcerer's power and the individual's health."

The uncertainty of such a curse was an issue. "Just think if someone gave you a gift whose sole purpose was to kill you?"

"That would be really unlucky," Dax said.

The room filled with contemplation as we absorbed the

potential implications of the spells we had discovered. Levy continued to make copies of any relevant spells, while Jaxson expressed his desire to find a spell that could induce paranoia, possibly explaining the mysterious behavior of Mr. Hastings. Unfortunately, we didn't find one, but I reminded Jaxson that our resident gargoyle, Hugo, could create the illusion of being chased. I wasn't implying Hugo was guilty, just that someone like Hugo could foster paranoia in a person.

Even with the list of possible spells, identifying the perpetrator would be a daunting challenge, particularly if the spell acted slowly. That would provide them with a strong alibi if they were in another town when the victim died.

Eventually, my eyes began to blur, and the spells all started to look alike. Since these people had lives of their own and had volunteered to help us, I felt guilty for keeping them this long.

I closed the book I was studying. "I think I've looked at enough for the day. What we've found gives us something good to go on. Let's hope that Harold's death was an isolated incident and that the evil entity responsible has no further victims in their sights."

"Yes, let's hope," Levy said.

Before leaving, I thanked my friends once again and offered to help put the books away. We might not have found all the answers yet, but we were determined to piece together the truth behind these deadly mysteries.

Dax shook his head. "I'll do it. Order is important."

That made sense. Neither Jaxson nor myself had any idea how the books had been arranged.

"I get it." I turned to my familiar. "Come on, Iggy."

He gave Camila a little peck on the cheek and then came over.

"I'll walk you out," Levy said.

Once he escorted us to the exit, I gave him a hug. "Thank you for always being here for us."

He smiled. "If I wasn't, my grandmother wouldn't let me forget it."

I knew that wasn't true. He liked the mystery of it all.

Jaxson held out his hand. "I appreciate you letting me sit in. It was quite enlightening."

"You're always welcome. Good luck with the search. Call if you have any questions."

I smiled. "We will."

We climbed into the car and took off. "Where to next?" Jaxson asked.

"I'm thinking we need to speak with Priscilla Primm. I don't think she had anything to do with Harold's death, but If she was in his shop often enough, she might have seen signs of his decline in the last few weeks or so."

"Do you know where we can find her?"

"That's where you come in."

Jaxson chuckled. "Got it. You want me to use my mad computer skills."

"Yup."

Once at the office, it didn't take Jaxson long to find Priscilla's home address. "Her social media site says she works from home, though I don't know what she does for a living."

I didn't think it mattered. "I say we see if she's there."

"I'm coming with you," Iggy said.

"Okay, but why would you want to? You might be bored."

"I know, but you said you didn't know if she was a witch or not. I could talk to her and see if she answers me."

I lifted him up. "That's a great idea."

Since Witch's Cove was a small town, it only took ten minutes to find Priscilla's apartment complex.

"Let's hope she's home and is willing to answer a few questions," Jaxson said.

"If she won't talk to us, it won't look good for her," I said.

Jaxson knocked, and Priscilla answered. "Yes?"

I hadn't met her, despite our town being small. "I'm Glinda Goodall, and this is Jaxson Harrison. I imagine you've heard about Harold Hastings' passing?"

She sucked in a breath. "Yes. It was tragic. His shop will be missed."

His shop, but not him? Interesting. "We're hoping you might be able to help us with something about Harold since we heard you visited his shop. May we come in?"

She hesitated. Inviting two strangers inside would be intimidating. Iggy must have sensed her concern, because he chose that moment to stick his head out of my purse. "Hi, there. I'm Iggy."

She leaned over. "He's so cute. What's his name?"

So much for her being a witch. "Iggy."

"Hi, Iggy. Sure, come on in, though I don't know what I can tell you. I rarely spoke with Mr. Hastings outside of his shop."

"That's fine."

She motioned us inside. The furnishings were rather old-fashioned despite her being in her forties. Her coffee table was an antique and was bordered by two velvet couches. Several bookshelves that contained old-looking tomes covered most of one wall. The dining room table was cluttered with her computer, which sat next to a pile of books and papers. It looked like what I imagined a writer's home would be.

"Excuse the mess. I'm working," Priscilla said.

"I get it. You're a working author. I wish I had the talent to write," I said. That was the truth. I bet my stories of murder and mayhem could be bestsellers.

"What are you working on?" Jaxson asked.

She shook her head. "It's silly really. I mean, I live in Witch's Cove, so I should know more about magic. My story is a fantasy romance, but my experience with romance as well as magic is rather limited. That's why I was visiting Mr. Hastings so often."

"I don't understand." I didn't want to give away that I was pretty sure I knew why she was in his shop.

"Mr. Hastings had a book in his store. It was called *The Enigma Stone*. I'd heard it was the definitive book on magic and spells. If I had such a book, I could add a lot of authenticity to my story."

That was the same book that Professor Eccleston wanted. "Did you buy it?"

"No. Mr. Hastings said it was from his personal collection. I'm not sure why he had it in the store if it wasn't for sale." Her lips pursed.

I shrugged. "I suppose if people learned about the book, they might stop in his store just to get a look at it."

"Maybe." Priscilla didn't sound happy, but was it enough to kill over?

"What did the book look like?" If we were able to get inside the shop, I wanted to check to see if it was still there. It might not have the name prominently displayed.

"It was old with a green leather binding." A small smile crossed her lips. "It really was lovely. A true work of art."

"Maybe the book will be donated to the library for all to see and use." I had no idea what would happen to any of Mr. Hastings' possessions. It was possible Charles would inherit everything, but considering their strained relationship, he might not care about antiques and donate what he couldn't sell.

"That would be wonderful. I know it would help with my research."

"One more question," I said. "Did you notice Mr. Hastings' health decline in the last few weeks?"

Priscilla's eyes widened. "Yes! I even mentioned it to him, but he said it was just seasonal allergies."

If someone had said that to me, I wouldn't have worried about it much either. "When was the last time you saw him?"

She shrugged. "I couldn't say for sure. Maybe two or three days before...his death."

Either Priscilla was a good actress, or she liked the man. Sure, she was angry—or rather highly disappointed—that Harold wouldn't sell or lend her the magic book. I could understand that. But she seemed too gentle to pay someone to kill for a book. I was pretty sure our own library had some books on magic—not to mention the Internet was filled with spells. Whether any of them worked, I didn't know.

"By any chance, did Mr. Hastings seem nervous of late?" Jaxson asked.

She looked off to the side. "Not really. I would say more irritable than anything else, but that could have been because he wasn't feeling well. He lived alone, and that can be tough on a person. I should know."

Since Priscilla was much younger than Mr. Hastings, it seemed highly unlikely the two of them would be an item. Besides, I didn't get the sense she was looking for a relationship.

"I'm sure you heard that he didn't die of natural causes."

She blew out a breath. "I heard that, but who would want to harm an old man? Mr. Hastings was nice."

"I didn't know him that well, but we're trying to help the sheriff find out. If you can think of anything Mr. Hastings said that would help us figure it out, let us know." I stood.

"I will."

Once she let us out, I was a little disappointed. I wasn't sure we'd accomplished much. Again.

"Your thoughts?" Jaxson asked.

"I think she's innocent. I didn't see anything that looked like *The Enigma Stone* on her dining room table. If she couldn't understand Iggy, it seems unlikely she is a witch. For the moment, I'd say she is not our killer."

"You don't find it odd that both Priscilla and Professor Eccleston were interested in the same book of spells?"

"Yes, but does it mean anything?"

"Let's go back to the office. I want to do a bit of research on the book. It might give a clue what the killer wanted."

Jaxson was often able to find things out that I thought were impossible. "After you do that, we should ask Steve if we can look inside the store. If we can't find that book, then the killer might have it."

"Let's do that."

CHAPTER 9

To my surprise, there was very little information on this Enigma Stone book. If Jaxson couldn't learn about it, I wonder how Professor Eccleston found out about it. Maybe he visited the store often and had seen the book.

When we entered the sheriff's department, Pearl was there, knitting away. She looked up. "You're back!"

"We are. Is Steve here? We have some news about the Hasting's murder."

Her eyes widened. "No. He got called out on something else. Would Nash do?"

The deputy might be better. "Absolutely."

"Then go on back."

Nash didn't have his own office, which was a shame since he was a talented law officer in his own right. His desk was located toward the back of the main area. Nash looked up and grinned. "You find the identity of the killer yet?"

"Funny. No, but we do have some information."

Nash pushed back his chair. "Let's go into the conference room."

That room was soundproofed. It needed to be with the queen of gossip sitting not far away. "Sure thing."

Once we sat down, I let Iggy out of my bag. He lifted his arm and waved but said nothing since Nash couldn't understand him.

"What have you learned?" Nash asked.

I told him about our trip to Levy's library. "We found a few spells that could have been responsible for Harold's death, but I'm not sure exactly how that helps us."

Nash nodded. "Anything else?"

"Yes." I went through our discussion with Priscilla Primm. "She said Harold hadn't been feeling well for a little while. That could point to the one spell that gradually harms the person. The problem is that the killer could have been in another state when Harold died, making his capture difficult."

"Even worse," Jaxson said, "is that if it's the spell that involves an artifact, who's to say if anyone else won't be harmed by it?"

"Good point," Nash said.

"Here's something I found odd," I said. "Two people were curious about the same book at Harold's store: *The Enigma Stone*. I'm wondering if that book has anything to do with his murder."

"What's the book about?" Nash asked.

"I wasn't able to find much on it, but I'll keep digging," Jaxson said.

"Priscilla said it contains spells, which she wanted to learn about for her fantasy romance book."

"I see," Nash said.

"Have you checked Harold's shop?" I asked.

"We walked through the store, but everything looked to be in order."

"Would you mind if we check it out? I'm not saying I

could sense if there is some evil aura floating around the store, but if *The Enigma Stone* is there, it might provide some answers," I said.

Iggy scurried across the table. "If you can't sense anything, I bet Hugo or Genevieve can."

"Excellent point."

"What did Iggy say?" Nash asked.

"He suggested we see if Hugo or Genevieve are free to look in the store. Being gargoyle shifters, they possess abilities that I don't have. They might be able to sense if evil is present."

"Even if I said it would be unorthodox to allow so many in the store, they could just teleport in without permission, so sure, ask them."

"I will."

Nash pushed back his chair. "Let me get the key to the store. How about seeing if your two friends want to join us? And then meet me in front of the antique shop."

"Sounds good." I gathered Iggy and placed him in my purse. Seeing Hugo would be fun for him. If Genevieve wasn't able to be there, we'd need an interpreter for our mute gargoyle.

After saying goodbye to Pearl, we headed down the street to the Hex and Bones. Bertha was behind the counter. She waved and came over to us. "How's it going?"

"Good, but we need some help from Hugo or Genevieve."

Iggy crawled out of my purse and down my leg. "Hi, Bertha. Bye, Bertha."

She chuckled. "Hugo's in back," she called after Iggy. "As is Genevieve," she told us once Iggy scurried away. "Did you find out anything about the spell used on Harold?"

I told her how we'd visited Levy's library. "We have a few possibilities, but a few things point to a book called *The Enigma Stone*."

Her eyes widened. "That can't be."

"Why?"

"Legend has it that *The Enigma Stone* tells of its ability to grant its possessor unparalleled magical ability and wisdom."

"That's not good if it gets in the wrong hands," I said.

"The book is smart. Those with dark magic can't even read it. The legend has it that only those with a pure heart and an unwavering commitment to using magic for good can access the book's true potential."

"That cuts my theory to shreds of it being used to harm Harold then," I said.

Bertha held up a hand. "As I said, it's only legend. But if Harold said he possessed it, I think he was either lying or was duped into believing he had the real deal. For ages, people have been searching for it. I doubt Harold possessed the real *Enigma Stone*. Chances are that someone duped an old man."

"We should still see if the fake edition of *The Enigma Stone* is in Harold's store. Not sure exactly what that would mean, but we should look," Jaxson said.

"Yes." I turned back to Bertha. "That's why we needed Hugo or Genevieve. We mistakenly thought the book could be used for evil. I might not be able to sense the evil, but I'm hoping Hugo or Genevieve can. There also could be some artifact in there that sends out vibes that were able to drain Harold of his energy and eventually his life."

"Good idea. Go back and ask them," Bertha said. "I'll be curious to know what you find out."

"Any idea who could be behind this?" I asked.

"Sorry. I asked around but didn't get far."

"Thanks for trying."

We headed to the back room where we found Iggy with Hugo and Genevieve. They both looked up, but only Genevieve smiled. Hugo still struggled with his emotions.

"Iggy told us what you need," Genevieve said.

"About that. There's been a slight miscalculation on my part." I told her what Bertha said. "The fact remains that we need to find out if there is anything in the antique store that is emitting a magical vibe that could kill someone."

Genevieve smiled. "Say no more."

One second she and Hugo were there, and the next they weren't. I hoped that when they teleported to the antique shop no one saw them just appear out of thin air. If they did that, this person would have to be looking through the storefront window.

Iggy crawled up to me. "What are you waiting for?"

"Impatient much?" Sheesh. I picked him up. "Let's make sure the deputy doesn't mess with anything."

"Hugo won't let him." Iggy had great confidence in his friend.

When we made it to the antique store, Nash had left the door ajar. I stepped inside, sad knowing that Harold Hastings would never be behind the counter again.

Even though Nash, Genevieve, and Hugo were inside, there were dust particles dancing in the rays of the sunlight that filtered in through the partially covered front window. There was an intangible sense of hope and magic that still covered everything.

"Glinda, are you okay?" Jaxson asked.

I jerked my attention back to the task at hand. "Yeah, sure. It's just sad that Harold is gone."

I couldn't help but look around at everything the man had collected. Shelves lined with weathered books, ornate clocks, and delicate porcelain figures stood as silent guardians of history's secrets.

What drew my attention were the few items that seemed slightly out of place, almost as if Harold had left in a hurry without straightening up.

"What should we be looking for?" Nash asked.

"*The Enigma Stone*—or rather what claims to be that book." I then faced Hugo. "Can you and Genevieve sense an evil spell on a book or artifact anywhere in the store?"

Hugo nodded. He and Genevieve methodically walked around the store, checking out all of the books and the knickknacks. The rest of us tried to find this book that Harold kept closely held, only we didn't find it.

"Nothing evil is here," Genevieve announced after a thorough search.

I was disappointed. "I guess that means there was no evil artifact sent to Harold that was meant to weaken him."

"Unless someone stole *The Enigma Stone*—or rather what they believed to be the real book. If we go by what Bertha says, the real book's worth is invaluable," Jaxson said.

"The one person, besides Priscilla, who showed interest in it was Professor Edgar Eccleston," I announced.

"Would you like us to look in his house for it?" Genevieve asked.

"To be thorough, we should do that. If he did take the book, and that book had a spell on it, then Mr. Eccleston might be ill."

"Do we have his address?" Jaxson asked.

"No, but I bet the college would know it." I looked over at Nash. "Could you call Palm Ridge Community College? Mr. Eccleston is a professor there. If you say he might have been exposed to something deadly when he visited our town, they might give you his address."

Nash nodded. "I can see why you're a good sleuth, but I won't need to lie. A request from the department should suffice. I'll need to call from our office, however. Do you need to see anything else here before I lock up?" he asked.

"No."

Genevieve and Hugo disappeared. "I wish they wouldn't do that where anyone can see them," Nash said.

"Good luck controlling them." They would behave for a while and forget.

Iggy, Jaxson, Nash, and I went back to the sheriff's department. When we reached Nash's desk, I heard Genevieve's voice in Steve's office. Really?

"Let me see what she and Hugo are up to," I said.

"I'll wait and get the address from Nash," Jaxson said.

I knocked on Steve's door and entered. To my surprise, Steve was there, and Genevieve was giving him the lowdown.

He looked up. "I see I'm gone an hour, and you've managed to waylay my deputy."

"It was for a good cause," I shot back.

"From what Genevieve tells me, you found a spell at Levy's library that might be the one used to kill Harold?" He didn't sound all that convinced.

"We found several spells. We're just following up on this one. I needed Hugo and Genevieve because they are capable of sensing evil vibes."

"Evil vibes?" Steve held up a hand. "Never mind. What's your next step? I know I might not know magic, but I am the sheriff and would appreciate being kept in the loop."

This was the same issue we always ran into. The problem was that sometimes we had to act on something right away.

"I thought Jaxson and I could visit the professor. While we ask him questions about *The Enigma Stone*, I was hoping Hugo and Genevieve could cloak themselves and search for it. I doubt he'd display something that valuable on his coffee table."

Steve inhaled. "Fine, but if they see it, please leave it where it is. We want to do things by the book as much as we can."

I didn't need to remind him that since the killer was a warlock, he wouldn't be tried in a human court of law. No telling what mind-bending things a powerful warlock could do to a jury. "Fine."

Genevieve nodded. A minute later, Nash came in and handed us the address. "According to the office, the professor has been on sick leave."

"Uh-oh. For how long?" I asked.

"I didn't ask. Is it possible the professor took this book that he thought was the real deal, and it is killing him too?" Nash asked.

"If I said yes, it would just be a guess." I looked over at Genevieve. "Do you have any idea what we could do with such a book if it was killing people? I mean, how does one destroy something that evil?" I asked.

"I've never tried to destroy anything magical before."

That stunk. "We have no idea if the professor is a warlock. I hope he is, because if he isn't, that means that this artifact might target anyone near the item. Since *The Enigma Stone*—or rather a fake version of the book—is not in the store, it seems logical to assume this book is the artifact that is imbued with some kind of curse."

"What's the plan?" Steve asked, sounding worried.

CHAPTER 10

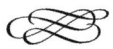

"We need to speak with Professor Eccleston, not only to make sure he has *The Enigma Stone*, but we have to be sure he doesn't just have a cold," Jaxson said.

Steve nodded. "Okay, but please don't accuse him of murdering Mr. Hastings. If he is guilty, he will be very dangerous."

Iggy popped his head up out of my purse. "Don't worry, sheriff. Hugo will make sure nothing bad happens to them."

Steve held up his palms. "Just be careful, that's all."

"We will." I showed the address to Genevieve. "Do you need to see a map?"

She smiled and then tapped her head. "Built-in GPS."

Before I could ask her if that was a joke, she and Hugo disappeared. And no, I wasn't surprised anymore by her antics.

Jaxson turned to me. "Ready?"

"Yup."

Once back in the car, I put the address in my GPS and told Jaxson where we needed to go. Palm Ridge was the next town over, and the professor didn't live far from the junior college.

A car was parked in his driveway, implying he might be home. The two-story home was a typical Florida stucco home. It was well-maintained and was on the upscale end of things.

"Let's do this," I announced. Even with having our two gargoyles nearby, I was a bit nervous.

Iggy told us that he'd say something to see if Professor Eccleston was a warlock. Knowing that would help us assess the situation better.

When we approached the front, the curtains were drawn, which made me wonder if he was home. Since we were here, we knocked.

No one answered. Darn.

"He's home," Iggy announced.

"How can you tell? You haven't suddenly developed X-ray vision, have you?"

"You're being funny. No. The television is on low. Knock again."

The man might not have answered because he thought we were from the school wondering if he really was ill. I knocked once more. "Profession Eccleston. We're here about Harold Hastings. Can you open up, please?" I asked.

I thought a female voice might be less threatening. Something scraped across what seemed like a wooden floor. The door eased open a bit. Oh, my. The man looked like death warmed over. He was not only wearing a plaid bathrobe and slippers, his nose was raw, and his hair—what there was of it —was uncombed.

"I am so sorry to disturb you, Professor Eccleston, but did you hear that Harold Hastings was murdered?" I asked.

I hoped Edgar wasn't the murderer, though if he tried to attack us in his weakened state, Jaxson could take him out—

magic or no magic. Not only that, I suspected Hugo and Genevieve were here. Darn. I should have asked Iggy if he could sense them. Too late now to ask.

"The antique shop owner was murdered?" Edgar Eccleston's face turned even whiter if that was possible.

"I'm afraid so. We believe he had a book at his store that was emitting poison. It was called *The Enigma Stone*. By any chance, did you touch it?"

Eccleston stumbled backward and then turned around. He dragged his fingers through his hair. "Oh, no. Oh, no."

When he dropped onto the sofa, I figured that was our invitation to enter. The room was very poorly lit, and the air smelled of sickness. It might not be all that safe for us to be here, let alone Iggy.

"Can you excuse me for a second? I need to put my pet in the car." I didn't need an ill iguana. Iggy had never had a cold before that I could remember, but there was always a first time.

Iggy popped his head up. "Pet, indeed. I'm not susceptible to that kind of magic."

Sheesh. I hope Mr. Eccleston wasn't a warlock. I didn't need him to hear what Iggy said.

"Magic, did you say?" he asked.

So much for pretending the book had been laced with poison. In truth, I wasn't sure how it worked—just that magic had been involved. "Yes. Here is what we know."

Jaxson and I detailed how Iggy found Mr. Hastings dead under the pew in the church where we were about to be married.

"I'm so sorry that the body interrupted your wedding."

"We'll have the service at another time. Right now, we want to concentrate on Mr. Hastings. We believe that a spell slowly made him weaker and weaker."

"I didn't put a spell on anything. I liked Harold. We both had a love of old things."

That made sense since the professor taught Ancient History. "We're not accusing you of anything."

Just then Genevieve appeared, holding a green leather-bound book. From the shocked look on the professor's face, he thought he was seeing a ghost. Or was he shocked to see that Genevieve had found his precious book—one he might have stolen?

"Who are you?" Eccleston's voice trembled.

"I'm Genevieve. I can teleport." She waved the book. "This is not the real *The Enigma Stone*. That one has never been found, or so my sources tell me. Did you steal this?"

Way to antagonize him, Genevieve. We were here to learn something. That being said, I wanted to know the answer to her question.

"No, of course not. Harold sold it to me."

Oh, how I wish Penny were here. She'd know if the man was telling the truth or not. "We believe someone put a curse on the book and sent it to Mr. Hastings, knowing he'd be drooling over having it in his possession. I admit it looks like a good replica, but from what I've learned, it isn't real."

The professor's eyes widened. "Is that why I've been so sick?"

"We believe so. If you stay close to the book for much longer, it might kill you, just like we believe it did to Harold." Yes, I might be stretching the truth, but it was possible what I said was true.

His mouth gaped open, and then he closed it. "How do I know you are who you say you are? How do I know Harold didn't hire you to get this valuable book back?"

Oh, boy. I didn't blame him for being skeptical though. "Call the sheriff's department in Witch's Cove. He'll tell you

Harold was murdered and that I am a witch who learned about the spell from a credible source."

Edgar picked up his phone. "What's the number?"

"Maybe you should look it up so you don't think we're trying to scam you," I said.

He nodded. It took him a minute to get the number. When he called, he asked about Harold first, which I thought was a good sign. "I see. And these young people here should be believed?" He looked over at Genevieve. "She did. Just appeared out of thin air. Okay, thank you," he said and then disconnected. "I guess you're legitimate. Now what?"

"Sir, did you really buy the book from Harold? Or did you *borrow* it?" I asked.

"Fine. I *borrowed* it as you so politely put it. I really did plan to return it, but then I became ill."

"Genevieve, can you and Hugo take that book someplace where no one will be affected by it? But don't destroy it. Yet," Jaxson said.

"We'll find a place for it, but it will have to be destroyed at some point," she said.

I blew out a breath. "I wish I knew how long the spell lasted. Whoever cursed this book had to realize that it wouldn't take long for someone as old as Harold to die."

"Am I going to die?" Edgar Eccleston's voice cracked.

What was I to say? "I hope not. How long have you had the book?"

"Only three days."

"That meant the book wasn't in Harold's possession for the last couple days of his life. I'm surprised he didn't improve." I said that mostly to make the professor feel better. I honestly had no idea what we were dealing with.

"Who did this to Harold?" Eccleston asked.

"I wish I knew. Do you have any ideas? Did Harold mention someone was out to get him?"

Eccleston shook his head. "No. We only talked about history—and magic."

The man leaned back against the sofa, looking as if meeting with us was taking a toll on his health. "Is there anything we can get for you?"

"No. My daughter comes over after work and helps me."

"Has she been ill?" I hoped this book wouldn't kill anyone else.

"So far, no, but I will warn her."

I grabbed Jaxson's hand. "Call the sheriff's office if you think of something that will help," I told him.

"I will."

Even though the book was gone, I wanted to get out of the house as quickly as possible. Back in the car, I called Levy and put him on speaker.

"Glinda. Do you have news?"

"I think so." I explained that we believed someone put a spell on a book that was in hot demand. "Turns out the book itself is most likely a fake, but no one seems to be aware of that fact. Anyway, a professor of Ancient History at Palm Ridge Junior College wanted it, and when Harold wouldn't sell it to him, he stole it."

"Don't tell me he's sick too."

"Sadly, yes." I explained how Genevieve and Hugo came—cloaked of course—and found the book. "I haven't spoken with Hugo yet, but I'm pretty sure they'll say the book is cursed. My question is, how do we remove the spell?"

"That is really tricky. We'd have to know exactly what spell was used in order to remove it. I think the easiest—or rather the safest—method is to do a purification spell. That would require collecting herbs, as well as locating some crystals and a few other items. But again, we need to know which spell was used in order to know which herbs are needed."

"That means we have to identify the killer," I said.

Jaxson squeezed my leg. "Even if we find the killer, what are the chances he or she will confess and tell us which spell was used?" Jaxson asked.

"Why is nothing about solving murder cases easy?" Yes, I was being silly.

"You'll figure it out," Levy said. "If you do learn the nature of the curse, let us know. We'll figure out a way to remove it."

"I appreciate it." I disconnected and then turned to Jaxson. "Now what do we do?"

"We haven't exhausted all of our suspects yet. Meaning, we need to find Alistair Brooklyn and Joseph Andrews. Since we know that Alistair is also in Palm Ridge, we should visit him," Jaxson suggested.

"I don't know where he lives exactly. Do you?" I asked.

"No. "That's the first thing I'll do when we get back to the office. Let's hope he didn't change his name when he moved here like Katie Altman did."

"Fingers crossed." Something seemed off. "Is it a coincidence that both the professor and Alistair live in the same town?" I doubted it, but I wanted to address all possible coincidences.

"Let's not discount anything."

It only took a few minutes to return to Witch's Cove. When we exited the car, Iggy hopped out of my purse. "I'm going over to check on Hugo."

"Okay, but if you feel light-headed or anything, you come home."

Iggy looked up at me. "Do you really think Hugo and Genevieve would actually keep the book at the Hex and Bones? That would be too dangerous."

"I hope you're right. While you're there, maybe you can find out where they are keeping it. We'll need it at some point to do the purification spell on it."

Iggy gave me what I considered a salute. He ran to the

pole, climbed up it, and then used the monkey bridge, which was basically woven rope, to cross the road. There was a very small door in the Hex and Bones that allowed Iggy to come and go since he wasn't able to open the door himself.

We climbed the stairs to our office. As soon as I stepped inside, a sense of comfort filled me. This was where I did my best thinking. "I'm getting out my whiteboard."

"Good idea. Let's hope there aren't too many Alistair Brooklyns in Palm Ridge."

"If there are a few, you can always send a picture of each to Gus. He'd be able to identify the man. That's assuming you can find an image," I said.

"You do your whiteboard stuff, and I'll handle the search for the address."

I smiled. "Yes, sir."

I was halfway through my list of suspects and their motives, when Jaxson stood and said he'd found the address for Alistair Brooklyn.

For some reason, I was nervous to meet the guy. "What if Mr. Brooklyn is some really powerful warlock who can put a spell on us? Should we ask Hugo and Genevieve to be our backup?"

"That's not a bad idea. I've been thinking that we could try to trick Alistair to see if he is guilty," Jaxson said.

"How do you plan on doing that?"

CHAPTER 11

"I thought you might know how to trick him into revealing something," Jaxson said.

"Me? That's Hugo's department," I said.

"Got it. We should let him handle it. If we tried to do something, we might be caught in one of Alistair's magic spells," Jaxson said.

"Remember, he might be innocent. Just because we have a list of suspects doesn't mean we haven't overlooked someone," I added.

"I know. As of right now, there are two left on our list—Alistair and Joseph Andrews. Though we can't forget Esmeralda Evergreen. Dolly must have had a reason to suspect that our nursery owner might be involved in Harold's death."

"Dolly's been known to exaggerate things for attention. I love the woman, but like all of us, she has her flaws. For now, how about we concentrate on Alistair? He seems like the most likely candidate."

"My money's on him too," Jaxson said.

"I know you have an address, but it's possible Alistair

skipped town as soon as he put the spell on Harold. His goal would have been fulfilled—assuming he's guilty."

Jaxson blew out a breath. "It would be the perfect crime. The killer could live across the country for all we know, put a curse on a book he knows that Harold would drool over, and then mails it to him. Harold holds onto this valuable book and then dies."

I loved it when Jaxson thought outside the box. "Or Harold could have ordered the book from some dealer, and our person of magic could have snuck into his store after hours and put a spell on it."

"That's always possible," he said.

"That brings up an issue for me. Considering Harold is this big antique expert, how didn't he know the book was a fake? *The Enigma Stone* is famous—or so Bertha believes."

Jaxson shook his head. "Denial maybe? Think about it. You receive this package in the mail—whether from an unknown source or because you ordered it. It's something you never thought you'd see in your lifetime. The book looks like the one you've seen on the Internet. The titles match. What's not to believe?"

I shrugged. "If Harold were alive, we could ask him."

"Since it's possible Alistair Brooklyn has regained his magical abilities, I agree with you that we should ask Hugo and Genevieve for backup," Jaxson said.

"I'll call Genevieve." I dialed the Hex and Bones Apothecary, and Andorra answered. "Hey, Andorra. It's Glinda."

"What's up? You want me to send Iggy back?"

I told her about our search for Harold's murderer. "Since he might have a fair amount of power, could you see if Hugo and Genevieve can stop over at the office?"

"Sure thing."

We chatted a bit more about what she was up to, and then I disconnected. Less than a minute later, Genevieve, along with Hugo, who was carrying Iggy, showed up at the office.

"We have the book in a safe place if that's what you need to know," Genevieve said.

"That's great, but we need your help. Again."

"Sure. What is it?"

Jaxson and I told her we'd like to visit Alistair Brooklyn, assuming he's still in Palm Ridge. Since he might be the killer, we'd like a little protection. I then gave her the address.

"Hold on. We'll check to see if he's home," Genevieve said a second before they disappeared.

"That will save us a trip," I said.

It wasn't long before she and Hugo reappeared.

"Your man is in his house. Alone. We did a quick sweep of the place. We found some paraphernalia like the stuff Bertha sells in the store, but not much else."

"Meaning he's doing spells?" Jaxson asked.

"It seems so."

I turned to Iggy. "I think you should stay here for a change—or visit Aunt Fern while we go speak with him."

"Why?"

"This Alistair guy is a warlock. What if we spook him, and he tries to do a spell on us?"

Iggy rolled his eyes—or his best estimate of eye-rolling. "Hugo will be there."

Hugo walked over and picked up Iggy. He then petted him, implying that nothing would happen to his good buddy. "Okay. But you hold onto Iggy, okay?"

Hugo nodded. And then they were gone. I hoped Iggy knew to keep quiet while they were at Alistair's home.

We climbed into our car and once more headed back to Palm Ridge. Finding Alistair's home was easy. It was a one-story wooden structure that had seen better days. It was possible that once he moved from Oakfield to Palm Ridge, he worked for lower wages. Ugh. I don't know why I jumped to conclusions without any facts. I had no way of knowing how he lived before.

"How are we going to approach him?" Jaxson asked.

"We say we heard that he knew Harold when they both lived in the Panhandle and wondered if he could give us some background on the man. We're here to learn who killed Harold."

"Got it. We go in with the mindset that Alistair is completely innocent. We can't even hint that we think he might be involved."

I chuckled. "I hope I'm a good actress. If we have the chance to interview him again, I'll remember to have Penny with us. She's so good at spotting a liar."

"That's a good plan."

When Jaxson knocked, the curtain parted, and a face peeked out. If I had been Alistair, I would have installed a peephole in the door. He eased open the door. "Yes?"

"Alistair Brooklyn?" I asked.

"Who are you?"

He was cautious. Good. I told him our names. "Harold Hasting's body was found under a church pew when Jaxson and I were about to marry."

"So? What does that have to do with me?"

"You were acquaintances in Oakfield. We were hoping you could give us some background information on Harold. Normally, the sheriff's department leads the investigation, but since I'm a witch, and our sheriff is not a warlock, he asked if I'd help."

"Harold was killed by a witch or a warlock?" Alistair said, fighting a smile.

"Yes. It was a spell put on a book in his possession. It killed him. Sadly, someone stole the book, and it is doing the same to him. We need to stop this trail of deaths." Okay, only one person had died, but I wanted to make him feel guilty if he was involved in any way.

"Maybe you should come in."

I'm glad he understood that discussing this in the open might not be smart. We went inside. If I had to guess, Alistair was in his mid-sixties. I didn't sense any evil vibes from the man, not that I knew if I would..

While I couldn't see Hugo, Genevieve, or Iggy as they were cloaked, I assumed they were close by.

"Sit down and tell me what you know," Alistair said. "Please."

I thought we were interrogating him. "We don't know much. That's why we're here."

"How did you know I was in Palm Ridge?"

Telling as much of the truth as possible usually worked. "We spoke to Harold's son to see what he might be able to tell us. Since he hadn't been close to his father for the last few years, he wasn't able to tell us much, but he gave us the names of a few of his friends. One of them told us about you."

"I can guess who that might be. Okay, so you found me. Now what?"

I couldn't quite tell if he was being defensive or bored. "What kind of man was Harold?" I asked.

"The worst kind."

The man didn't pull any punches. I decided to follow suit. "Why? Because he took away your magic?"

The man winced. "In part, yes, but he did a lot more damage than that to others."

The word damage implied something evil. "Can you give me an example? I didn't know Harold all that well, but everyone claimed he was a nice old man."

Alistair laughed. "The man was never nice. He was into dark magic."

Since my friends were there to prevent anything bad from happening, I decided to go on a limb. "Were you dark magic buddies?"

Alistair jumped up. I will admit that I stiffened. "Who have you been talking to? I have never dabbled in the dark arts. If I had, I might have been able to stop Harold." He practically shouted at us.

Whoa. Now, Alistair was claiming that he was the good guy? From his red face, he might be telling the truth. Oh, how I wish Penny were here.

"Mr. Brooklyn, can you give us an example of something that Harold Hastings did that was bad?" Jaxson asked.

"Oh, I can tell you a lot, but the worst was when Harold stole my older sister's memories from her—to the point where she didn't even remember me. It took showing her old photo albums to make her believe we were related. Even now, she's not quite back to normal."

"That's absolutely horrible. Why would he do that?" I asked.

"He wanted me to join him in a very unsavory adventure. I declined, so he took my sister's memories of me away."

"Excuse me, but I thought he removed your magical abilities," Jaxson said.

"He did that later. After he took away my sister's memories of me, Harold was willing to give me a second chance if I reconsidered. When I told him no the second time, he said I was useless to him. That's when he took my magic."

"I might have killed him for that," I mumbled to myself.

"I heard that," he said. "I wanted to kill him, only I didn't have the power."

"Is your power still gone?" I asked.

"Not all of it, but it's nowhere near where it was. Maybe

in time, it will return."

"Mr. Brooklyn, why did you move close to Harold?" Jaxson asked.

"To keep an eye on him."

That didn't make a lot of sense to me. "Weren't you afraid he'd do more damage to you?"

The man shrugged. "Short of killing me, I'm not sure what he could do."

"Sir, what did you hope to gain by keeping an eye on him?" Jaxson asked.

"I have friends who could try to stop him if he went on another rampage," Alistair said.

"Did he?" I asked. "Go on another rampage?"

"Not that I heard about. I probably should have returned to Oakfield, but I like it here in Palm Ridge. As far as I knew, Harold never learned that I lived here."

"Did you ever visit Witch's Cove in order to spy on him?" I wasn't sure how what he said would help us, but I wanted to be thorough.

"A few times. I asked around to see if there were some unexplained events that had occurred, but I didn't hear of anything."

He seemed to be telling the truth. "In your searches, did you learn of anyone else who might have wanted to kill him?"

"No."

He said that a little too quickly. I glanced over at Jaxson, who nodded. This interview was at an end. I stood. "Thank you for your help. It gives us a better idea as to what kind of person we are looking for."

"I'm glad I could help."

Jaxson and I left. I was curious to find out what, if anything, Genevieve and Hugo had learned, so we headed back to the office.

"What are your thoughts?" I asked Jaxson.

"I'm still trying to process it. I'd like to do a little research to see if what he says is true or not."

"About his sister, you mean?"

"For starters, yes," he said.

"I'm sensing you didn't believe him."

"I think Harold might have been the bad buy in this scenario, but I'm not so sure Alistair isn't guilty too. If Alistair was this super benevolent warlock, why would Harold approach him in the first place? If someone with dark magic came to you and asked you to do something bad, you'd say no, even if they threatened to harm me."

"I might not go that far," I said. "However, I don't know if I can do dark magic. I'm not sure a witch has a choice. Either you can do good magic or bad magic. At least that's my understanding."

Jaxson glanced over at me. "I love you, but please don't ever give in and turn to the dark side—assuming you could. No good would come of it."

I had to think about that. "So you're saying, we shouldn't cross him off the list, right?"

"Exactly."

When we arrived at the office and went upstairs, I wasn't surprised to find our invisible party there. "Did you learn anything? I asked.

"Not at first," Genevieve said.

"He made a phone call right after you left," Iggy interjected.

"To whom?" I asked.

"We don't know." Genevieve looked over at Hugo. That implied that Hugo could have used some kind of magic and dug into Alistair's mind to learn who it was.

"What did he say? You could hear that much." I probably said that with a bit too much impatience.

CHAPTER 12

"The conversation between Alistair and his caller was short. All he told the person was that they needed to be cautious. Then he hung up."

That was disappointing. "That's not exactly incriminating."

"No, but there must have been something you said that bothered Alistair."

"Let me grab something to drink. I need a moment to think. Anyone else want something?" I asked.

Since the only other human in the room was Jaxson, he lifted his hand. I ducked into our small kitchen and quickly made two cups of coffee. Once I carried them out, I grabbed my whiteboard. "I believed Alistair for most of it, but I had the sense that, at times, he wasn't being honest."

"I agree," Jaxson said. "I couldn't tell you which part I didn't believe though."

For the next few minutes, we listed the conversation in bullet-point form. Surprisingly, Hugo seemed to have the best recall. Of course, either Iggy or Genevieve had to translate.

The one good thing to come out of the rehashing of the conversation was that Jaxson said he could check up on some of the facts.

"Maybe we should tell Steve what we learned and see what progress he's made with Esmeralda, aka Katie Altman," I said.

"How about we talk with the Oglethorpes first?" Jaxson suggested. "Remember, Steve asked that we get their opinion on our nursery owner."

"You're right. I forgot. The problem is that it's kind of late." I looked at my watch. "Their flower shop will be closed."

"Then we'll go first thing tomorrow morning."

"Works for me. I'm hoping that if Esmeralda is aware the Oglethorpes have magic, she might let her guard down with them," I said.

"Let's hope," he said.

"Hugo and I are going to head out then. Let us know if you need any more protection detail," Genevieve said with a smile.

"Will do."

Iggy looked up at Genevieve. "Thank you."

"You bet, buddy." Then they disappeared.

"How about dinner at the Tiki Hut?" I said.

"Works for me."

I DIDN'T SLEEP ALL that well last night as I couldn't help but go over all of our suspects and their motives. Most had a good reason for wanting Harold dead, but was the person with the best motive the killer? Were there extenuating circumstances that we were unaware of? Ugh. I really disliked it when the puzzle pieces didn't fit.

"Ready to visit our florists?" Jaxson asked.

"I am." I turned to Iggy. "We're going to see the Oglethorpes. Do you want to come?"

"No. I'll stay here and think."

I chuckled. "Think about what?"

"The case. You two aren't as sharp as you usually are. Someone's got to think clearly."

I worked very hard not to laugh. "We appreciate it. I hope you figure something out." To be honest, Iggy had often provided some key insight into the case.

"I always do, but if I'm not here when you come back, I might check on Bandit."

"You do that." Bandit was a raccoon who now resided at the Hex and Bones Apothecary, because his host had been murdered. The problem was their friendship often caused Iggy to end up in trouble.

With Iggy seemingly happy to stay put for a bit, Jaxson and I headed out. Since the Oglethorpe flower shop was just down the street, we walked there. When we entered the shop, I automatically inhaled the sweet aroma of the flowers. I always loved coming here.

"There they are. The happy couple—or you will be once the nuptials are complete." Sheila Oglethorpe, who was behind the counter, smiled.

"We're happy no matter what," I assured her.

"Of course you are." Sheila came around the counter and hugged me. "What can I get for you two today?"

Since no one was in the store, we could talk privately. "I'm guessing you've heard about Harold Hasting's death?" My mom surely would have discussed it with her since they were best friends.

"Of course. Such a tragedy. Do you have any leads?"

"Some." While I trusted Sheila not to blab, for her sake, it might be better not to tell her everything.

"Are you here because you think I can help?" Sheila asked. "I didn't know Harold very well."

"That's okay. Esmeralda's name was brought up in the course of discussion," I said. "What can you tell us about her? I know you buy a lot of your flowers from her nursery."

"I do. She has talent when it comes to growing things, though I suspect she uses some magic to get her amazing results," Sheila said.

"I personally don't have a problem with that as long as it doesn't harm anyone."

"I don't either. I feel bad that shortly after she arrived in Witch's Cove about three years ago, she basically drove The Green Earth Nursery out of business. The thing is, her plants are superior."

That was sad in a way. "I guess some would call it progress. I'm almost surprised no one tried to sabotage her."

"Winslow was the owner of the other nursery. He might have tried to do something had he been a warlock. I doubt he had any idea how she was managing to grow such beautiful flowers, however."

We were getting off-topic. "Not that I think Esmeralda had anything to do with Harold's death, but did you see any behavioral changes in her of late? Like was she angry or concerned about Harold's declining health in the last week?"

"Funny you should ask. She actually asked if I had noticed Harold's weakened state. Her expression appeared sincere, but I had the sense she was almost happy he wasn't doing well. I mentioned it to Tim, but he thought I was imagining things."

I made a mental note of that. "What do you know about her personal life? Is she married? Where is she from? Do you think she is basically a nice person?"

Sheila blew out a breath. "She's from Florida. I know that,

but I didn't ask which town. As far as her being married, no, but I recall her saying something about being engaged once. It didn't work out, but I don't know any details. As for children, if she had them, they aren't with her now. To be honest, I never pressed her on her life's details. Esmeralda and I have a professional relationship, but that's all."

"I appreciate the information. If you run into her, see if there is anything else you might be able to learn from her."

"Ooh. You mean you want me to be a spy?"

I chuckled. "Whatever works. Just don't mention that we were asking about her. If she had anything to do with Harold's death, we don't want to spook her."

"I got it."

Since we'd finished picking Sheila's brain, I suggested to Jaxson that we grab some breakfast at the diner before checking in with Steve.

"Do you think Dolly knows something else?" Jaxson asked.

"She was the one who told Steve about Esmeralda in the first place. Usually, Dolly doesn't spill the beans unless she has some kind of proof. The problem is that our gossip queens like to one-up each other. I hope Dolly didn't make anything up."

"Let's find out."

The diner was fairly crowded for a weekday morning, but our favorite booth in the back was available. Since there was an ongoing crime investigation, I figured Dolly would be the one to wait on us for the sole purpose of getting more dirt. She loved being in the know.

Sure enough, she said something to one of the waitresses and then came over. "How are my two favorite sleuths?"

"Working hard. Before we share, I wanted to say thank you for everything you did to help with the wedding preparations. You and the other ladies went above and beyond."

"Nonsense. We had a blast decorating. I can't remember the last time we had a big wedding. And you two are special in this town. Why, if you didn't have your agency, things would be mighty dull around here. So, tell me everything."

She didn't really expect us to tell her everything. Even Dolly was aware that she couldn't keep things to herself. "We're looking at a lot of suspects. The sheriff told us that you thought Esmeralda Evergreen might have harmed Harold. Why did you think that?"

She had Jaxson scoot over so that she could sit next to him. "First off, she came in here one day fit to be tied."

"Because Harold Hastings sold the book of plants out from under her?" I asked.

"That's what she claimed, but I had the sense he'd done something else."

"Did she say what he'd done?" I asked.

"Esmeralda wasn't specific, but she said something about him doing something underhanded back home."

I sat up straighter. "Back home? Don't tell me she's from Oakfield, Florida?"

Dolly shrugged. "Sorry, I didn't ask."

"But you had the sense that she and Harold had known each other before she moved here?" Jaxson asked.

Dolly pressed her lips together. "I couldn't say one way or the other, but that's what I suspected."

That added a nice twist to things. "Have you ever seen her go off the deep end before?" I asked.

"No, but to be honest, she's not a frequent visitor of the diner."

"Okay. We'll speak with her, but if she does come in...."

Dolly held up a hand. "Don't you worry about that, sweetie. Old Dolly here can get the most reluctant person to tell me some tidbit of gossip."

I laughed. "You are the best."

Dolly stood. "So what can I get you two to eat?"

As if she didn't know what I would order. I practically lived there. "Chocolate chip pancakes for me topped with whipped cream. I'm a bit stressed."

"I don't blame you what with the wedding being postponed and Iggy swallowing the ring."

"Add in finding the dead body, and I'm on overload."

"I hear you. You want coffee, I presume?" she asked.

"Always."

She turned to Jaxson, pen ready to write down his order, though I was pretty sure she didn't need to take notes.

"For you, handsome?"

"I'll have two eggs over easy and an English Muffin—I'm splurging—and my coffee black."

"I'll put the order right in."

Once Dolly went back to the counter, I turned to Jaxson. "What do you think? Is Esmeralda involved?"

"People get angry all the time at injustices. It doesn't mean she'd kill over a book of plants being sold out from under her. That being said, the fact she might have known Harold before moving here brings up a lot of questions. Had she had a run-in with him before and moved here to keep an eye on him like Alistair did? Maybe Harold did something bad to her, too, assuming Alistair was telling the truth."

I smiled sweetly. "I guess you'll be doing some research after breakfast."

"I will."

"I GOT SOMETHING," Jaxson said. He'd been at his computer for quite some time once we returned from breakfast.

"What is it?" I put down the whiteboard and walked over to his desk.

"Dolly was right. Esmeralda, aka Katie Altman, is from Oakfield, Florida."

"Interesting."

"Here is the intriguing part. I looked on her social media site, which has been inactive since she moved here. There are only a few pictures of her, but look at her back then."

I studied the images. "That's her? Are you sure? Maybe there are two Katie Altmans."

"I thought that at first too. This one has long brown hair and is rather chunky. I know she is standing in a nursery, but even so, she doesn't seem to have taken good care of herself."

That was an understatement. "The Katie Altman who's here is a blonde, but that can be attained with hair dye. What is striking is that she is now rail thin. Plus, she has a different name. I wonder how Steve learned of her real name?"

"He probably did some checking. Though it's possible she told him."

I had to think. "Is it possible that she wanted to disguise herself so that Harold wouldn't recognize her?"

"If that were the case, why wait all those years to kill him—assuming she's guilty?"

"It's not like she'd tell us if we asked her," I said.

"No, but she is a powerful witch, so if we interact with her, we need to proceed with caution."

"That goes without saying. Let's inform Steve what you found out and see what he thinks."

CHAPTER 13

Jaxson, Iggy, and I walked across the street to the sheriff's department. When we entered his office, the aroma of fresh-baked cookies filled the air, causing my stomach to grumble. Oh, how I loved Pearl's cookies. She'd been baking—that, or she went next door and bought a bunch from the coffee shop.

"Come to say you've solved the case?" Pearl asked with a grin.

"We wish. We have checked out several suspects, but no one stands out as being the guilty party. Is Steve in?"

"He is, but take a cookie before you go in. I'm tempted to eat the whole batch. They smell so dang good."

"They look divine. I don't mind if I do." I picked up one and then another. I never could resist sweets.

Naturally, Jaxson resisted, displaying his admirable willpower.

With cookies in hand, I knocked on Steve's door, and upon hearing his invitation to enter, we stepped inside.

"I hope you have some leads," he said.

"We might. We spoke with Professor Eccleston," I began.

"He called and asked if you two were who you said you were. Is he a good candidate for having killed Harold?" Steve asked.

"Not anymore." We explained that he'd *picked up The Enigma Stone*—or rather the book he believed was the authentic book—without asking permission."

"So he stole it. Got it. Are you saying the book is a fake?"

"Yes, however the same spell on the book that killed Harold is now killing the professor. That's why we don't think he's guilty."

Steve whistled and then grabbed his yellow pad. "We'll cross him off the list." He looked up at us. "If this book is harming people, we need to defuse it quickly."

I almost laughed at his wording for removing a spell. "Genevieve and Hugo have it somewhere safe where no one can be harmed by it. However, we do need to do a purification spell on it as soon as we learn the proper incantation."

"From what Glinda says, to do that, we need to find the murderer and ask them what spell they used," Jaxson said.

"I see." The sheriff scribbled more notes. "Anyone else you suspect?"

"Yes." We told him about Alistair. "If you recall, he is from Oakfield, the same town as Harold."

"I remember him."

"Anyway, according to Alistair, Harold Hastings was a bad man. Harold was the one who used dark magic. In fact, if we can believe Alistair, Harold put a spell on Alistair's older sister so that she wouldn't remember him."

"Why would he do that?" the sheriff asked.

I explained that Harold wanted Alistair to help him in an unsavory deal. "Alistair turned him down. As a result, Harold removed the sister's memories and took away most of Alistair's powers."

Steve whistled. "That's bad. And a good motive for murder."

"I know, but I don't know how much of Alistair's powers have returned. I'm not sure he's capable of putting such a spell on *The Enigma Stone*. He'd say no if we asked him, and if he is the murderer, we can't trust him to tell us the truth."

Steve jotted down more notes. "I see."

"After we left Alistair's place," Jaxson said, "he made a phone call. We know because our cloaked friends stayed around to see what he would do."

"That was smart. Could they tell who he called?" Steve asked.

"No, but he told this person to be careful. We aren't sure what he meant by that."

"Do you believe what he told you about Harold being a dark warlock and stealing the sister's memories?" the sheriff asked.

"For the most part, but Jaxson is going to do more research."

"Good."

We still had one more suspect. "Can I ask how you knew that Esmeralda Evergreen's real name was Katie Altman?"

"Ah, yes. I wasn't sheriff when she arrived in town, but if you recall, when one wants to open a business, one needs to apply for a license."

The light dawned. In most cities, the town hall handled it, but not in Witch's Cove, apparently. "I had to do that. That means Sheriff Duncan took her fingerprints."

"Yes. Normally, as soon we have them, we do a quick background check, but apparently, Sheriff Duncan was a little lazy—that or I couldn't find his report."

"Color me surprised. Not." The man was a bad sheriff. He accused Jaxson of murdering the deputy.

Steve fought a smile. "However, after her name was

brought up as a suspect, I ran her fingerprints through the system. They came up as Kathryn Altman from Oakfield, Florida. That's how I found out."

"That's good police work, Sheriff. But if Katie's fingerprints were in the system, it means she had a record," Jaxson said.

"Yes. The fact she was from Oakfield had me investigating further. Turns out she was brought in for questioning for a few incidents that involved vandalism. If she was guilty, the police weren't able to prove anything. That might be because she used some kind of magic—again, assuming she was guilty of the crime."

"That is the benefit of our craft," I said. "We can get away with a lot of things. Most criminals with powers are counting on that."

"But they didn't count on our magical sleuth to figure things out," Steve said.

I chuckled at that name. "Anyone who commits a crime in Witch's Cove, believing that their magic won't be discovered, is not very bright."

"I agree," Steve said

"Were any of these vandal attacks directed at Harold?" Jaxson asked.

"No, and I checked. I'm not saying she's innocent, but do you have any other suspects?" he asked.

"No, but I want to talk with Esmeralda."

The sheriff shook his head. "Even if she isn't involved in Harold's death, she could be trouble." Steve held up his hand. "That being said, you are well aware that people can change. She might have wanted to move away from Oakfield in order to get a fresh start."

He was being too generous. "That may be, but to be safe, I'll once more ask Hugo and Genevieve to cloak themselves and come with me when I speak with her."

"Can a witch sense that our two gargoyles friends are near?" he asked.

"I know I can't."

Iggy poked his head up out of my purse. "I usually can sense when Hugo is close by."

That wasn't good. "Maybe it's because you two have a special bond," I said.

"Maybe."

"Do you really want to tip her off that we suspect her though?" Jaxson asked me.

"I have a plan for that. I thought I'd ask Penny to go with me when I speak with her. We'll be two women looking to buy some plants. That's all. I'm not sure what we'll ask Esmeralda, but Penny will know if Ms. Evergreen is telling the truth."

The sheriff nodded. "I'm not sure what you can learn, but be careful."

I smiled. "Always."

"Oh, I almost forgot," Jaxson said. "I found an old picture of Katie Altman that was maybe ten years old. She was a brunette back then instead of a blonde. She wore thick black glasses, but I don't recall if she wears them now. Also, she was rather overweight."

"Interesting. I wonder if she just decided to go to a gym and get contacts, or if she was trying to change her appearance so Harold wouldn't recognize her?" Steve asked.

"That's what I wondered," Jaxson said.

"I have an idea. I'll see if Penny can pretend that she recognizes Katie." I shook my head. "On second thought, that might be too dangerous for her," I said.

"You could ask Genevieve to do it. I don't think there is anything a witch can do that would harm a gargoyle shifter," Jaxson said.

"That's good thinking. I guess I'll have to keep you around, after all." I leaned over and kissed his cheek.

Steve cleared his throat. "Keep me up-to-date on what you learn."

As if we didn't always? Okay, sometimes we thought it better if we waited a bit before telling him.

"Oh, I forgot to ask if the toxicology report came back on Harold?" I asked.

"It did. No evidence of poison—at least none of the ones they tested for."

"That corroborates my theory of a magical poison. Thanks," I said.

Once we left, I suggested we stop at the Hex and Bones. It would make Iggy happy, and I needed to speak with our resident gargoyles anyway.

"I'm game."

As soon as we stepped into the Hex and Bones, Iggy immediately crawled out of the bag. He didn't need to tell me where he was going.

"Let's chat with Bertha while Iggy gives Genevieve and Hugo the lowdown on what we need to do," I said.

"Good idea."

We walked over to where Bertha was straightening up the spell books on the table. She turned around and smiled. "I hear you two have been busy."

"You can say that."

"Did you ever learn what kind of spell was used on Harold?" she asked.

"No. I trust Genevieve told you that Professor Eccleston who was interested in *The Enigma Stone* is also ill?"

"Yes, what a shame. That spell must have been very powerful."

"How can one tell?" I asked.

"Often spells—especially dark ones—are only directed at

a particular person. I honestly thought that once Harold died, the spell would lose its strength."

I hadn't known that fact. "Any idea what kind of spell it might have been?"

"I'm afraid not. You said you were going to speak with Levy. Of anyone, he would know—unless Gertrude might."

"I'm hoping a general purification spell will work if the original spell isn't known. However, it would be helpful if we knew which spell was used on the book," I said.

"Don't hold your breath," Bertha said. "That's like asking a magician to divulge his secrets."

I was worried about that. "I suppose worst case, we can ask Hugo to make the person tell the truth."

Bertha smiled. "First, you have to figure out who it is."

"So true." Someone came into the shop. "I'll let you go. I need to speak with Genevieve and Hugo about some protection duty."

"I have to say that having them here has given all of us some peace of mind," Bertha said.

Just then Bandit the raccoon wandered out from the back room with something in his mouth. "You were saying?"

Bandit was cute and meant well, but he often ended up in trouble.

Bertha laughed. "I'll admit he has a penchant for trying to open things that he shouldn't touch."

I was happy that Iggy was usually good about not messing with my things. "I'm sure Genevieve and Hugo can have a talk with him."

"I might ask them."

When we went to the back room, Hugo was holding Iggy, and Genevieve was listening to what my familiar had to say.

She turned around and smiled. "I hear you want our protection services."

"I do, but first I need to see if Penny is free. She's so good at telling if a person is lying, though there was a case or two where even she was fooled."

"I'll ask her," Genevieve said a second before she disappeared.

"I was going to do that," I announced.

"Penny will understand," Jaxson said. "She knows that Genevieve is rather impetuous."

"That she is."

It didn't take long before Genevieve returned. "Penny would be delighted to go with you. She was quite excited actually. She told me she loves being a spy."

I laughed. "We won't be spying. However, I was wondering if maybe you could go up to Esmeralda at one point while we're speaking with her and call her by her real name: Katie Altman?"

"Sure, but why?"

"On the off chance that she came to Witch's Cove to spy or keep tabs on Harold. Having people know her real name should make her uncomfortable, assuming she had something to do with Harold's death."

Genevieve's eyes opened. "You think she killed him?"

I didn't want her to treat Esmeralda as a murderer. "I honestly couldn't say. We have no proof, but she might let something slip if she thinks we know she and Harold are both from the same town."

Jaxson told her how her appearance had changed. "You might say you went to high school together, assuming you can find out what classes she took. She grew up on Laramie Street if that helps."

"I'll figure something out." Genevieve turned back to me. "And you think that if she knows we are aware of her real name, she'll freak?"

"Possibly," I said. "After Penny and I leave, stay around in your cloaked form and see if maybe she makes a call. If she is guilty, she might do something foolish."

"I love solving crimes," Genevieve said.

"It isn't solved yet, but hopefully, it will be soon."

CHAPTER 14

"Iggy, do you want to go back to the office with Jaxson?" I asked.

"No, I'm going to stay with Hugo. That way, when he's protecting you, I can watch."

I never liked it when Iggy was in possible danger, but as long as Hugo held onto him, he'd be okay. "Fine, but don't leave Hugo's side."

"I won't."

When Jaxson and I left, I pulled out my phone and called Penny to make sure she could get away now.

"Are you kidding? When Genevieve told me that my skills were needed, I was so happy."

I smiled. "How about I come and pick you up now?"

"I'll be ready."

Once across the street, I opened my car door.

"Are you sure you don't want some backup?" Jaxson asked.

He was so sweet. "I think Hugo can handle little old Esmeralda—or should I say, Katie Altman?"

"Just be careful. She might realize you are really there to

find out about Harold. No telling what kind of revenge she might exact."

I stood on my toes and kissed his cheek. "I am a witch. I'm not helpless, you know."

Jaxson dipped his chin. "Are you going to try to cloak yourself so you can run away or something?"

Cloaking took effort and required me to say a small spell. I wasn't like Hugo and Genevieve, who could disappear in a flash. "No, but I'll figure something out."

I had built up a small arsenal of spells, but those took time to perform. "I shouldn't be too long—unless I really do buy some plants."

"Or chat with Penny."

"Or that." After a quick hug, I rushed out, slipped into my car, and headed north to Penny's place.

My best friend was standing outside her house. When I stopped, she hopped in. "This is so exciting. Tell me everything."

I chuckled at Penny's enthusiasm. I did the best I could to summarize what we'd learned. "Too often, I was sure we'd found the killer, but so far, each of them has me doubting it. Either he or she didn't possess the ability to put a spell on this fake book, or the motive is weak."

"Esmeralda is your last suspect?" Penny asked.

"For now, yes. We just scratched off the professor from our list, because he fell ill to the spell," I said.

"Is it possible he purposefully poisoned himself to throw the suspicion off?" she asked.

"Hmm. That would be a great alibi. The professor could have decided to keep the spell on the book just long enough for him to be sick but not enough time for him to die."

"I guess his name needs to go back on the list," she said.

"I guess so."

When we arrived at the plant nursery, there weren't many cars in the lot.

"Do you know if Esmeralda has people working for her?" Penny asked.

I never thought about that. "I don't know. How about we wander around, and when we see her, we'll go up to her."

"And ask her what?"

"Since she might know that I run an investigative agency, how about saying you need some plants that are good for growing in the shade? That way, it will look like I'm here to keep you company."

She smiled. "Smart. Sometime during our conversation, Genevieve will show up pretending to know her."

"Exactly."

"Let's do this." Penny pushed open her car door.

There were rows and rows of amazing-looking plants, some in pots, and others in the ground. "Do you see her?" I asked.

"I don't know her," Penny said.

"Blonde, pretty, around forty, and thin."

As if she could sense someone was looking to buy something, Esmeralda emerged from a small building on the property.

"That her?"

"Yes."

Esmeralda smiled and came toward us. I had to say she didn't look like a killer. In fact, she appeared very approachable.

"Welcome, ladies. How can I help you?"

It was now Penny's turn to do her thing. "My backyard is a mess, and I need some plants that will grow well in the shade."

"Not a problem. Come with me. I'll show you what I have."

As we followed Esmeralda, I wondered where Genevieve was. If she didn't show, poor Penny might be forced to buy some plants.

We were halfway through the small lecture on the best plants to use in the shade when a woman came over—a woman I'd never seen before.

"Katie? Is that you?"

Esmeralda, aka Katie, stopped and looked over at the woman. She then glanced at me and then at Penny. Indecision was written all over her face.

"Who are you?" she asked, clearly trying not to be rude, but failing.

"Sandy Cromwell from Oakfield Junior High. Why you are just as pretty now as you were back in school. If I recall, you used to wear glasses, right?"

"Sandy. Yes. Of course." Esmeralda turned to us. "If you don't mind, I need a minute. Look around while I chat with Sandy."

And then the two of them took off. Darn. When they were out of earshot, I faced Penny. "That stinks. We can't hear a thing. I wish I knew where Genevieve was. It's not like her not to show up."

Penny studied the woman. "How do you know that's not Genevieve?"

"What are you talking about? Does that woman look like our gargoyle-shifting friend?" I asked.

"Of course not, but if she can shift into a piece of stone, how do we know she can't shift into looking like someone else?"

That made total sense. Genevieve had so many talents I couldn't keep up with them. "It could be her, but that would imply in the span it took me to pick you up, she was able to find a picture of a junior high friend, age her, and then somehow look like her—either through amazing makeup or magic."

"All she really had to do was find the name and probably hope Esmeralda didn't ask her any questions about those times. I say we sneak out and hope that woman really is Genevieve."

"Works for me unless you really do need plants for your backyard," I said.

Penny smiled. "If I had to buy something to make it look good, I would have bought them. The backyard could use some sprucing up, but I'm good for now."

"Come on."

Esmeralda might have noticed we left, but customers probably took off without purchasing something all the time. The trip back to the Hex and Bones didn't take long. "What if that woman wasn't Genevieve?" I asked.

"I'm not sure it matters. When asked if she was Katie Altman, Esmeralda never answered. To me, it implied that she was trying to hide something," Penny said.

Penny had a good point. "We'll find out soon enough."

I parked in front of the Tiki Hut since the Hex and Bones Apothecary was more or less across the street. We headed that way and entered the store. Bertha was with a client and Elizabeth, her granddaughter, was helping someone else. She looked up and smiled. I waved and then headed to the back room.

Genevieve was there with Hugo and Iggy. "Genevieve, was that you at the nursery?"

She grinned. "It was. From the look on your face, I fooled you."

"Yes. If I wasn't expecting you, I never would have guessed it was you. Great make-up job."

"Thanks."

"Did you learn anything?"

"Some things. Katie eventually admitted she was Katie Altman, but we knew that. I told her I had come to town because I was now an antique dealer and heard that Witch's Cove had great antiques."

"Very clever," I said.

"Was she nervous?" Penny asked.

"Very. I think it was mostly because I could identify her."

"Did she ask if you knew Harold from back home?" I asked.

"She did. I said I remembered the name, but that was all. She seemed to be in a hurry to get rid of me."

"I don't think that incriminates her, but it doesn't prove her innocence either. Jaxson said he wanted to do more research. I'm hoping he found something," I said.

"If you need us for anything else, let us know." Genevieve smiled. "You know, I could pretend to be Harold come back to haunt her. That would freak her out."

I laughed. "That would be something to see. I will keep that in mind, though that in and of itself, might not prove anything."

Genevieve smiled. "I know."

Hugo handed me Iggy. "Come on, little man. Time to do some work—after we drive Penny home."

Once I took Penny back to her house, I thanked her again. "I might need your expertise in the future."

"Any time."

On the way back to town, we neared the church. It was then that I remembered the pencil the sheriff said had been in Harold Hasting's hand. "Iggy, I need you to check under the pew of the church."

"Why?"

"The sheriff said that Harold had started to write something. We assume it was the name of his killer, though how he would know who had put a poisonous spell on his book, I don't know."

"I can look, but what do you think I'll find?"

"I don't recall the sheriff being on his stomach examining the marking, though I was more concerned about you than the crime," I said.

"You're such a softie," Iggy shot back.

"Softie or not, I thought with your eagle eyes, you might see something."

"I can try."

He always responded well when I buttered him up. I pulled in front of the church and parked. "Let's see if Harold gave us a clue."

For the sake of speed, I carried Iggy inside. The light barely filtered through the windows, which might make it hard for Iggy to see. Good thing he had good eyesight..

I set him down. "Do you remember where you saw the body?"

"Oh, please." Iggy rushed to the pew and crawled underneath, his claws scraping against the hardwood floor.

I didn't hold out a lot of hope since the church was old and the floors were worn.

He must have spent a full minute under there. When Iggy emerged, he pranced up to me. "To the untrained eye, it looks like a straight line and nothing else."

To the untrained eye? "But you saw more?"

"Yes. The rest of the letter was very faint."

I waited for him to tell me the letter, but I knew Iggy well. "I suppose you're holding out for an extra serving of lettuce."

"I am."

I wasn't strict enough with him. "What was the letter?"

"It was an A."

I went through the list of suspects. "That could be Joseph Andrews, the man who had the deer problem, who we have yet to find, Alistair Brooklyn, the man whose sister's memory was more or less erased, or Katie Altman."

"Oh," Iggy said. "I guess that didn't help much."

"No, it helped a lot. We'll let Steve know and then see what Jaxson learned."

"Okay, but then I get my lettuce."

I chuckled. "I promise."

Upon returning to town, I parked and then went across to the sheriff's office.

Jennifer Larson was there. "Hey, Jenn. I have some info for the sheriff. Is he in?"

"He is. I'll let him know. Go on back."

When I knocked and then entered, Steve leaned back in his chair. "I'm beginning to wonder if you're going to ask the town to start paying you for your services."

"I am a sleuth, don't forget. Besides, I like to help."

"Good. What do you have?"

I went over how when Penny and I were talking to Esmeralda, Genevieve somehow managed to change her appearance to that of a junior high school acquaintance of Katie's. "When Genevieve asked if she was Katie Altman, our nursery owner became a bit flustered."

"Did she say anything incriminating?"

"Not really."

Iggy poked his head up. "Tell him about the mark on the floor under the pew."

"I'm getting to that." I then explained how Genevieve said that she came to Witch's Cove to look in the antique store. "Harold's name came up, but Genevieve couldn't say one way or the other if Katie had anything to do with Harold's death."

"The letter. Tell him about the letter," Iggy said.

"Iggy, you tell me," Steve said.

Iggy hopped up on his desk and described what he saw.

Steve pulled out his yellow pad and made a note. "That

could be one of several people, assuming the A was telling us the killer's name."

"That's what I thought. Jaxson is doing some more digging on our suspects," I told him.

Steve nodded. "I'll do the same. I'll give the sheriff in Oakfield another call."

"Cool." I pushed back my chair. "I'll be in touch."

"You do that," Steve said, clearly trying to hold back a smile.

CHAPTER 15

"Did you find any dirt on our nursery owner?" I asked Jaxson as soon as I returned to the office. "No pun intended."

"Not directly, but I'll tell you about it shortly. I decided to research the others a little bit more first. Before I share my vast knowledge, tell me how it went with Esmeralda." He winked.

I loved his sense of humor. "Let me get a coffee. This may take some time."

"Grab me one too," he said.

"And some lettuce for me."

"I will, Iggy."

I ducked into the small kitchen area and prepared the coffee. While I waited for the water to heat, I placed some lettuce leaves on a plate and carried it out to Iggy.

"Thanks."

After I made the coffee and took it out to Jaxson, I pulled up a chair and sat next to him at the desk. I went through the discussion with Esmeralda. "Before we could say much though, a woman showed up and asked if Esmeralda was Katie Altman from Oakfield."

"You're telling me some random woman came up and asked her that?"

"Turns out Genevieve went to Oakfield and looked up a picture of an old classmate. She was able to make herself look like this woman."

Jaxson's brows shot up. "Did she use makeup or magic?"

I smiled. "I think a little of both. Anyway, I don't think Katie gave away much, though Harold's name came up in the conversation."

"And?"

I shrugged. "Before she could ask anything else, Esmeralda said she had to take care of another customer and walked off. That customer might have been us, but I can't be sure since Penny and I had left."

"That does sound a little suspicious."

"I agree, but it's nothing the sheriff can act on. Tell me what you learned."

Jaxson scrolled to a page on his computer. "I learned that Alistair Brooklyn had a sister, but she died quite a while ago."

"I thought he said that Harold put a spell on his sister to erase her memory, but that she was slowly improving. That means he lied."

"Yes, though it's not out of the realm of possibility that he was referring to another sister—like a step-sister."

"Or Alistair might have had a girlfriend rather than a sister that pretended not to know him, and he was too embarrassed to admit it," I tossed in.

"That's as good a guess as any, assuming we believe he wasn't lying."

"Something doesn't ring true about it all, but I don't know what. We could ask him again, but I'm thinking he won't tell us," I said.

"Hugo can find out," Iggy said.

"That's true, though all evidence would be hearsay," I told my cute iguana. "Even though the guilty party will be tried in a magical court, I know Steve likes to keep things by the book as much as possible."

"I wish there was a way we could trace who Alistair called after we left," Jaxson said.

"I bet Steve could do it, but he needs a good reason—and probably a warrant. Right now, we don't have a good enough reason to even ask him. I think I'll see if Hugo and Genevieve wouldn't mind babysitting Alistair and Esmeralda to see if one of them does something suspicious."

"I'll go and ask," Iggy said.

"I appreciate that but calling will be faster." I pulled out my phone and called Genevieve. I explained that I needed some surveillance work done.

"We'll be happy to watch them. How long should we stay with them?"

Since neither ate nor needed to sleep, they could stay there a long time, but I didn't want to ask that of them. "How about until they go to sleep?"

"You got it."

"Do you know where—" I attempted to ask if she knew where they lived, but Genevieve had hung up.

They'd been to Alistair's house, but I didn't know if they knew where Katie Altman lived. Most likely, Genevieve would go to Katie's nursery and follow her home.

"Did you learn anything else?" I asked.

"I found Joseph Andrews. The last known address was in Georgia, but that doesn't really mean anything. He is a warlock, so he could have come after Harold."

"I wouldn't think a person would have waited a few years before taking revenge."

Jaxson shrugged. "If we use that logic, then Alistair and Katie are innocent too."

"Why would you think that?" I asked.

"In theory, it's been a while since Harold supposedly took away Alistair's theoretical sister's memory of him. Why wait?" he asked.

"I see your point, unless Alistair needed for his powers to regenerate. Not only that, a person of magic might not have known that he could create a spell that would make a person sick. I didn't know it was possible."

"You, my dear Glinda, aren't evil."

"That's true. I suppose that points the finger at Katie then," I said. "She wanted a book on plants. I understand being upset that he sold it out from under her, but come on. Would someone really kill over that?"

"I'm betting not, but think about it. Katie is from the same hometown as Harold. He comes to Witch's Cove. A year or so later, she comes to Witch's Cove. That can't be a coincidence."

"And she changed her name," I added. "Mind you the change in hair color, size, and vision correction might have nothing to do with wanting some kind of disguise. Though why change her name?"

"Esmeralda Evergreen is a great name for a nursery owner," Jaxson said. "She might have changed it simply because it would help her sell more plants."

"That makes sense." Darn, I wanted at least one of our suspects be the obvious killer.

"I think I'll focus on Joseph Andrews. None of the other suspects are jumping out at me," Jaxson said.

"Hugo will figure it out," Iggy said.

"That would be nice." Iggy believed his good friend could do anything. I hoped he was right. "But he's busy at the moment watching Alistair."

While Jaxson did more research on our last possible suspect, I went over to the whiteboard and filled in a few more ideas. Then Jaxson's cell phone rang.

"Pink Iguana Sleuths," he said. "Hey, Gus." Jaxson listened for a minute. "When? Uh-huh. Are you sure the information is accurate?" More silence. "Thanks for checking it out." Jaxson hung up.

"What did he say?" I asked.

"Joseph Andrews died three weeks ago. Car accident."

That was before Harold's death. "Did Gus say if he thought it might not have been so accidental?"

Jaxson shook his head. "Joseph was under the influence and ran a red light. I think we can cross him off the list."

"For sure." I tapped the whiteboard. "Jaxson, why again do we think that Harold's son is innocent? He is a warlock, remember, and we have no idea how powerful he is. If we're to believe Alistair, Harold was powerful, which means Charles could be too."

"For starters, he seemed shocked by his dad's death, though people can and do act. You keep thinking about it. I'm going to go to the post office to see if they have any records on whether Harold received a package about a week ago."

"A package? Do you mean the book?" I asked.

"Yes. We might be able to trace who sent it," he said.

"If the person was smart, they'd buy the book, put the curse on it, and then send it from a different location—other than where they live."

He smiled. "That's a good guess, but by speaking with the post office, I might be able to narrow things down."

"You know, we don't know how long he's had the book. He could have bought it three years ago!"

"I realize that, but I want to check anyway."

"Okay. I'll work on the motives for our suspects," I said.

Jaxson kissed me and then left.

"Do you think you can do all that smooching when I'm not here?" Iggy asked.

"Nope. If you don't like it, close your eyes."

Iggy turned around and hightailed it out the cat door, and I had to chuckle at his antics.

I went back to my whiteboard. It wasn't long before Genevieve and Hugo showed up.

"Hey," I said. "I thought you were going to stay around until Alistair and Katie went to bed."

"We would have, but we have news."

"Do tell."

As if Iggy could sense that his friends had arrived, he jetted through the cat door. "Hi, Hugo. And Genevieve."

Genevieve nodded. "Hello, Iggy."

"You were saying?" I prodded.

"Oh, yes. Katie called Alistair. When he answered, she addressed him as Uncle Alistair."

I sat there stunned for a moment. "Katie Altman is Alistair's niece?"

"Yes." She held up a hand. "I did a little sleuthing myself—none of which would be legal by your sheriff's standards, but I checked some records at the courthouse in Oakfield. Katie's mother was Alistair's sister."

"And that sister is dead." At least that was what Jaxson found out.

"Yes."

"I need to find out the dates of when those two came here." I picked up the phone and called Steve. I told him about Katie and Alistair being related.

"How does that help us solve this crime?" he asked.

"We're putting the pieces together. Can you tell me when she applied for her business license?"

"Sure. I'll look it up and text you."

"Thanks." I hung up before he warned me to keep safe, blah, blah, blah.

"What do you want us to do next?" Genevieve asked.

"How about doing a quick check on Professor Eccleston to see if he is still ill?" I asked.

"Sure." And then they disappeared.

"What can I do?" Iggy asked.

I smiled. "Just keep me company."

He waddled over to me and climbed up on the sofa. "Okay."

My cell pinged. "It's a text from Steve giving me the date for when Katie moved here."

"When was that?" Iggy asked.

"Almost three years ago." I wasn't sure why that was important though.

"Her uncle moved to Palm Ridge at that time, too, right?" Iggy asked.

"Yes. The question I have is why did he move to Palm Ridge and not Witch's Cove? That's assuming he wanted to be near his niece."

"Maybe he got a job in Palm Ridge."

"That sounds plausible."

The door to the office opened and Jaxson came in. "The book, as far as we could see, wasn't delivered to our post office."

I threw out a crazy idea. "Maybe it was sent to Palm Ridge."

Jaxson eye's widened. "You think Alistair is the evil one here? I thought his powers weren't strong enough."

"Or so he claims. I'm trying to keep our options open. Our two gargoyle shifters learned that Katie is Alistair's niece."

"How did I miss that?"

I shrugged. I explained what Genevieve did to find that

information.

Jaxson sat across from me. "Before we jump to conclusions, I think we need to speak with Charles again. He might be able to fill in some blanks."

"If we go there, I'd like to have Penny with us. That way we'll be more certain if he's telling the truth or not."

"That's a long drive—too long for tonight. Besides, if his wife and kids are there, he won't talk," Jaxson said.

I nodded. "How about we go tomorrow morning? Maybe we can ask Genevieve and Hugo to teleport us there. It will be a lot faster."

"That's for sure, though it might look odd if we aren't in a car."

"We can tell him the truth. It might make him be more honest," I said.

"Next time you see Genevieve and Hugo, ask if they can check to see if he's home first."

I smiled. "I like it."

Just as I was about to call them, Hugo and Genevieve reappeared. Iggy rushed up to Hugo who picked him up and smiled—a rarity.

"The professor is feeling a little better, but he really was ill. I believe he'll live though," Genevieve told us.

"Great. I think we can put him at the end of our suspect list."

"Tell Genevieve who's still on the list," Jaxson prompted.

"Joseph Andrews is deceased. Since he passed before Harold died, I'm thinking he's not guilty." I went through the other people.

"So, you're down to Alistair, Katie, and maybe Charles?" Genevieve asked.

"For the moment yes, which is why we'd like to visit Charles tomorrow." I then asked if she could check to see if he was home. If he was, could they teleport me, Jaxson, and

Penny there? "Of course, we'd like you and Hugo to be there just in case something goes wrong."

"Absolutely. What time?"

"Say ten?"

"We'll be here to escort you to Oakfield."

Hugo placed Iggy on the floor and disappeared. "What about me?" Iggy asked.

"Let's see what our friends say tomorrow. It might be hard to take all of us. We all have to be touching, you know."

"I'll sit on Hugo's shoulder."

I smiled. "That will work."

CHAPTER 16

"Ready to do this?" I asked Jaxson and Penny.

We wanted to pick Charles Hasting's brain in the hopes he could provide new information about his father as well as corroborate what we'd already learned about him.

Genevieve said he was inside. As for Iggy, he was cloaked with Hugo and Genevieve.

We walked up to the door and rang the bell. A few seconds later, Charles pulled open the door, and his shoulders sagged. "What do you want?"

Considering he wasn't exactly friendly, he might not be guilty. Why? Often times I found the guilty ones wanted to appear innocent. Charles didn't seem to care what we thought of him.

"We need your help."

His eyebrows rose. "I told you everything I know."

"Yes, everything we asked about, but we're hoping you can fill in a few blanks," I said. "Please?"

Charles stepped to the side and sighed. "Come in then."

While he didn't sound happy we were there, he didn't slam the door in our faces.

"This is Penny Carsted. She's a witch who is exceptionally good at detecting if someone is lying." I wouldn't mention the times that she'd made crucial mistakes.

"Is that necessary?" Charles asked.

"I hope not."

"Have a seat and ask me anything. While you may not believe it, I want to learn what happened to my father. We might not have seen eye-to-eye, but we were blood."

"I understand. Let me start by telling you what we believe to be true. Do you know Alistair Brooklyn?"

"I know of him. Why?"

"He said that your father was into dark magic. Is there any truth to that?" I asked.

"I've always suspected it. It's one of the many reasons why we didn't speak very often." He held up a hand. "When he moved to Witch's Cove, he swore he was finished with magic. Was he? I couldn't say."

I nodded. "We've not heard that he used any of his skills while in town."

"Then why was he killed?" Charles asked.

"We have a theory, but we'd like your input." I explained about Charles' dad wanting Alistair to be involved in something sinister. "When Alistair turned your dad down, your father took away—or at least weakened—Alistair's powers."

"Jeez. That's terrible."

Penny looked over at me and nodded, indicating Charles was telling the truth. "Alistair said that your father also wiped the memory of Alistair's sister to the point where she didn't recognize him."

Charles shook his head and grunted. "He did the same thing to me."

The man was pure evil if he did that. Doing it twice made Harold an even worse person—assuming it was all true. "Tell us what happened."

"It took a while after it happened before I was ready to believe it, but I think I've put the pieces together. Before I met my wife, I was dating a woman that my father didn't approve of."

"When was this?" Jaxson asked.

"About four years ago."

He was a fast mover if he'd already married and had children.

"I can see you're confused since I told you I had a family. My wife and I married three years ago. She already had two children."

"Thanks for clearing that up."

"My father tried to dissuade me from being with Katie. He said she was bad news, but I wouldn't listen. She was a witch: creative and hard-working. But she had a few run-ins with the law. Why that bothered my dad, I don't know. He was no saint as you've learned."

"I'm sorry to interrupt, but what was Katie's last name?"

"Altman."

"You dated Katie Altman? The same Katie Altman who moved to Witch's Cove and changed her name to Esmeralda Evergreen?" My voice cracked.

Charles' face paled. "I have no idea where she went after she left town, nor am I aware that she'd changed her name, but if you think she is the same person, she might be."

"Did you know Alistair was her uncle?" I asked.

"I'm sure I did, but when my father wiped my memory—or most of it—I forgot."

Jaxson pulled out his phone. "I downloaded this picture of Katie when she lived in Oakfield. Is this her?"

Charles looked at the photo, and his cheeks sagged. "Yes."

Jaxson explained how her fingerprints indicated her true identity.

Charles' eyes grew wide. "Are you thinking she had something to do with my dad's death?"

"You tell me," I shot back. "If, as you claim, you and Katie were close and your father erased your memory of her, I'd be mad if I were her. Or did I fill in too many gaps?"

"No, you are right." Charles dragged his hands down his face. "This is a nightmare."

"I trust Katie was quite upset when you didn't recognize her," I said.

"That's putting it mildly, but remember I had no idea who she was."

"Did she think you were trying to blow her off?" Penny asked.

"Yes. But she had photos of us together. The pictures weren't altered—at least they didn't seem like they were. In them, I looked happy. Really happy. We were engaged, according to her."

I couldn't imagine what I would do if suddenly Jaxson didn't know me. "How did you know your dad had erased your memory?"

"After Katie was able to convince me that I had a memory problem, I remember my dad doing a spell to bless us. Only the spell was not for that."

"Did Katie ever say she was going to get her revenge?" Jaxson asked.

"Not to me. Then again, I didn't want anything to do with her at that point. I had met Monica by then. Monica's my wife."

"How powerful of a witch was Katie?" I asked.

"I don't know. Part of my memory was jogged after seeing the pictures, but the rest is blank. Since I wasn't interested in her anymore, I didn't try to get to know her. Look, I wish I could help you, but that part of my life is a big black hole."

I stood. "Thank you for being so forthright with us."

"I would like to see justice for my dad. If Katie was responsible in any way for harming my father, she had good reason."

Too bad the law didn't work that way. "I understand."

As soon as we left, Hugo, Genevieve, and Iggy appeared. Since it wouldn't do to have a lengthy discussion on his front yard, I suggested we return to Witch's Cove.

A second later, our two gargoyle shifters returned us to our office. Since Hugo, Genevieve, and Iggy had cloaked themselves, hopefully, one of them had wandered about Charles' home.

"Did you see anything interesting while at his house?" I asked.

"I found something in his desk drawer," Genevieve said. "It was a *Congratulations on Your Wedding* card from his dad. It just said that he was happy he married a better woman."

"Eww. That's almost creepy," I shot back.

"It gives credence to the fact that his father might have put a memory block on Charles," Jaxson said.

"True. So what's our next step?" I asked.

"I don't know. Sadly, we have no real proof that Katie is guilty of anything."

"Then why did she move to Witch's Cove right after she found out that her fiancé didn't remember her?" Genevieve asked.

I wracked my brain to come up with a reason. "She learned there wasn't a lot of competition for a nursery in Witch's Cove? I know that's lame, but I got nothing."

"Do we know if Katie even had a nursery in Oakfield?" he asked.

I looked over at our two shifters. They shrugged. "We'll see what we can find out." And then poof.

Iggy looked up at me. "I wanted to go. Why didn't they take me?"

"If you are with them, then they can't smooch."

"Gross," he said. "I've never seen them do that, just so you know."

I'd just made that up. It bothered me to see him disappointed. "Thoughts, anyone?"

"Let's say that Katie was the one to put the spell on the book that killed Harold. The book had to reach his store somehow," Jaxson said.

Iggy climbed onto the sofa. "Who's to say the book wasn't always there, and Katie came in one night and put the spell on the book?" Iggy said.

"Excellent question. I wonder if Professor Eccleston would know?" I asked.

"Why would he?" Apparently, Jaxson wasn't seeing it.

"He might have visited often, and perhaps Harold bragged about coming into possession of the book."

Jaxson's eyes widened. "Impressive. Give him a call. I imagine he's home since Genevieve said he was still ill."

I retrieved his number and gave Mr. Eccleston a call. After asking about his health, I wanted to see if he recalled when Harold came into possession of *The Enigma Stone*.

"Let me see. I visited him two weeks ago, and Harold didn't mention anything about the book. Of all people, he would have said something to me about it since I was aware of how valuable that book was."

"When did you visit him again?" I asked.

"A week later. That's when he said he'd searched high and low for it, and eventually located it."

"So Harold bought the book. It hadn't been a present. Interesting," I mused.

"Wasn't he aware how rare the book was? I mean no one had been able to locate it up to that point in time." Something seemed off.

"It wasn't something I asked about. All I know is that he paid a lot for it," the professor said.

"When you *borrowed* the book, did it appear authentic?" Was it possible he had the real deal?

"I'm embarrassed to say that I wanted it to be real so badly that I didn't think to question if it was authentic."

"Last question since I know you aren't up to full health yet. Did Harold say who or where he ordered the book from?"

Edgar Eccleston hesitated for a moment. "I honestly don't remember."

"Thank you for your help."

"Thank you for realizing that the book had an evil spell on it. If you hadn't, I might be dead," the professor said.

"I'm glad we did." Then I disconnected. Since I had the phone on speaker, Jaxson and Iggy had heard it all. "Well?"

"We need to find that receipt," Jaxson said. "If we can tie it to someone on our suspect list, it will help take down the guilty party."

"Do you want to check out his store or his home?" I asked.

"Both," he said. "I think we should split up. Assuming they are willing, we could have Nash or Steve check Harold's house, and we could check the store. We'll need Iggy, Genevieve, and Hugo to do the real search."

"I want to be with Hugo!" Iggy said.

"That works. Let's see if the sheriff is willing to participate or if he thinks this is a wild goose chase." I thought it was a long shot, but we had nothing else to go on. "Come on, Iggy."

Before we made it out the door, Genevieve appeared. "Okay, I found out that Katie worked at a large nursery in Oakfield. The owner said she talked about moving and starting her own nursery one day."

"Then she might have come here for that reason," I said.

"Thanks, Genevieve," Jaxson said. "We need to keep an open mind then."

Genevieve nodded and teleported out.

"Darn. I should have asked her about helping with the search," I said.

"Let's see what Steve thinks first. Then we can ask her."

The three of us then left the office and crossed the street to the sheriff's office. Pearl looked up and smiled. "You must be psychic."

"Why is that?" I asked.

"Steve asked me to give you a call. He found something. He and Nash are in the conference room."

"Thanks." As we walked toward the back, I couldn't help but wonder what he'd found.

I knocked on the glass door and entered.

"That was fast," Steve said.

"We just came over to tell you what we found out."

"Then have a seat." On the far end of the room was a projector screen. "On the off chance someone snuck into Harold's store and did the spell, I got a hold of the security tapes for the last two weeks."

"Wow. I'm impressed. What did you find?"

Steve held up a hand. "Hold your horses. Even if I spotted my grandmother breaking into the store, it wouldn't necessarily mean she put a spell on the book."

"Because she's not a witch. I get it. So who did you see?"

The lights dimmed, and the footage appeared. "You tell me," Steve said.

CHAPTER 17

If I were to rob a place, I'd do it at night. That's why it made sense that the footage was dark. High tech cameras had yet to be installed in Witch's Cove.

From the side of the frame, two figures approached Harold's shop. Steve stopped it. "Can you tell who it is?" he asked.

I had to squint, but the faces were turned to the side. Iggy climbed onto the table and moved closer, though I wasn't sure that would help. "Not really," I said.

"It looks like a blonde lady," Iggy proclaimed.

"How can you tell? The person is wearing a baseball cap with her hair tucked underneath."

"I have good eyes," my familiar stated.

"I thought it looked like a woman." Nash was responding to my comment since he didn't hear Iggy.

"You might be right since the person is only a few inches taller than me. Plus, she's very thin and walks like a woman," I said, becoming more confident the longer I watched.

"That was my thought too," Steve said.

"The other person looks a lot older," Jaxson tossed in. "He's limping a little, almost as if he has a bad leg."

I tried to think of someone who limped. Too bad most of the people we spoke with had generally been sitting down.

"Let me continue to play it. We'll get a quick glance at the faces in a moment," Steve said.

We watched for another few seconds. Maybe because I had Katie Altman on my mind that I swore that one of the people was her and the other was her uncle. "It really looks like Alistair and Katie."

"I agree," Jaxson said.

"Me three," Iggy added.

"We thought that too," Steve said. "If it is Katie and her uncle, it would only prove that they broke into the store. It doesn't mean they put a spell on the book."

"We have more information that might at least explain why Katie and Alistair would want Harold dead. And yes, it doesn't prove anything, but this case might have to be built on circumstantial evidence."

Nash almost smiled. "What do you have?"

Between the three of us, we told him that Joseph Andrews, the man with the deer problem was dead. We went through the entire conversation with Charles about how his dad had put a spell on his own son because he didn't like his choice of women. "And guess who Charles was engaged to before the dad interfered?" I asked.

"Don't tell me it was Katie Altman?" Steve asked.

"Yup."

"No wonder she wants revenge," Steve said. "Now we just have to prove it. While I could arrest her for breaking and entering, without Harold around to bring charges, she could say he told her to meet him at the store. When he wasn't there, they could say they thought he fell ill or that he just forgot to show up."

Sadly, Katie probably could come up with a good excuse. "What's the time stamp on the breaking and entering?" I asked.

"Two in the morning."

"Hardly a common time for a meet-up," I said.

"Agreed. Did you two learn anything else?"

"I spoke with Professor Edgar Eccleston."

"The man who *borrowed* the poisoned book?" Steve asked.

"Yes. Harold told Edgar Eccleston that Harold had ordered the book himself. No one sent it to him."

"We're hoping to find the receipt either at his home or his store," Jaxson added.

"What good would that do?" Steve asked.

"If I could tie the receipt to either Katie or Alistair, it would help prove they were involved. Not only that the person who sold him the book claimed it was an original. If nothing else, they scammed Harold," he said.

"The person who sold him the book could be someone we've already decided isn't guilty," I said. Like his son.

Jaxson glanced my way. "Let's not get ahead of ourselves."

I often did that. I'd crossed people off our list of suspects in the past and later learned that they were the guilty party. "Fine."

"Would it help if we found ingredients to a spell in Katie or Alistair's possession?" Nash asked.

"Maybe, assuming we learn what spell they used. However, the ingredients would have to be something rather rare. Even if you did find everything, it really won't prove a lot in and of itself."

"Got it."

"Do you think Genevieve and Hugo could help us?" Steve asked. "They were good at detecting spells and such before."

"I'm sure they'd love to help. I imagine they can search

quickly, though I really don't understand the full extent of their abilities."

"Hugo can find anything." Naturally, that comment came from Hugo's biggest fan.

"I'll call them," I said.

"Tell them to walk down the street."

"Got it."

When I called Genevieve, I explained that we needed their help in finding a receipt for the book that had the spell placed on it. "Steve has asked that you not teleport to his office."

"Spoilsport." And then she laughed. "We'll be right there."

"They are on their way," I said. "Steve, have you been to Harold's house yet?"

"Not yet."

"Bertha said he is kind of a hoarder."

"Are you volunteering to look through his place then?" he asked.

"Ah, no."

Steve huffed out a laugh. "I didn't think so."

When Hugo and Genevieve showed up, we broke the group into teams. Nash would escort me and Genevieve to the store, while Steve would take Hugo, Jaxson, and Iggy to Harold's house.

"Call if you find anything," Steve said.

"Will do."

As we walked down the street to Harold's store, Genevieve stepped closer. "Do you really think you can find one particular receipt?"

"I'm hoping that's where you come in," I said.

"How?"

"Can't you channel one of your talents and find it?"

Genevieve chuckled. "I'm not all-powerful. Maybe you

could do a spell that would help you visualize where he might have put it," she said.

I had no idea such a spell existed. "It's worth a try. But if I do a spell, I'd need your help."

"Of course."

When we reached the store, Nash let us in. "Where do we begin?" he asked.

"How about you take the computer, I'll look in his drawers—assuming they are unlocked—and Genevieve can search the room?"

"Sounds good," Nash said.

We spent the next fifteen minutes looking through his books and drawers. "The man had no sense of order," I complained.

"I agree. His file system on his computer makes no sense either," Nash told us.

We didn't seem to be making much progress. "How about you guys keep looking while I go to the Hex and Bones to see if Bertha can scrounge up a spell that will help me find this item?" I asked.

"Sounds good," Nash mumbled as he continued to search through the mess Harold called a computer.

"Do you need me?" Genevieve asked.

"I think Nash could use you here. Call me if you find it."

I hurried to the Hex and Bone. Andorra was managing the desk, but I didn't see her grandmother. That might make this more difficult.

"Hey. I heard our two gargoyle shifters have been hard at work," Andorra said.

"They have been amazing. Right now I need a location spell. Any idea where we could find one?"

"As a matter of fact, a woman came in not long ago asking for one. I think we found three. Let me show you."

Andorra and I headed over to the table of spells. She

located several. "The key is whether we have all of the ingredients in stock," she said.

I read all of them. "I think this fits what I need the best."

Andorra smiled. "Let me see what the backroom holds."

While she searched for the ingredients, I carried over the book. I'd need her to make a copy of the spell. While I had been working on my spells with Gertrude, I wasn't all that confident I would be successful. However, if I didn't try, I'd never know.

Andorra came out with a tray of things. "You're in luck."

"Super. Can you copy the spell for me?"

"Sure thing."

When she returned, I paid her, placed the spell and ingredients in the bag, and left for Harold's shop. When I entered, Genevieve and Nash were still searching.

Nash looked up from the computer. "You find something?"

"I did. Fingers crossed it works."

Genevieve came over. "Let me see. I love spells."

"No pressure, and no guarantee this will work."

"You won't know until you try." This comment came from Nash.

I placed the items on the counter and spread them out. "How about when I read the spell, you hand me what I need?" I asked Genevieve.

She looked over my shoulder and read the ingredients. "No problem."

I placed a wooden wand next to the mortar and pestle. Next, I lit five candles. I had the sense these were more for ambiance than anything—at least that was what Gertrude claimed. I placed the petals and crystals on the other side. The other items weren't really items but were things I was to conjure in my mind. "I'm ready."

With the spell in hand, I began.

. . .

> *"By moonlight's glow and magic's might,*
> *I seek the clue that's hidden from sight.*
> *With whispered words and mystic art,*
> *Reveal the receipt, the vital part.*
> *Eyes of newt and herb of thyme,*
> *Add to this spell, oh enchanted rhyme.*

I STOPPED and motioned for Genevieve to hand me both the eyes of newt and the thyme. I then placed them in the mortar and pestle. Using the wand, I began to stir while continuing the spell.

> *A candle's flame, flickering bright,*
> *Illuminate the path of night.*
> *In mortar's embrace, let's combine,*
> *Crystals and petals, gifts of time.*

Genevieve quickly handed me the crystal and petal—rose petals in this case.

> *Stirring 'round with a wooden wand,*
> *Weave the magic, respond to my demand.*
> *A sprinkle of stardust, a dash of glee,*
> *A pinch of laughter, as it should be.*
> *From shadows deep, my senses keen,*
> *Lead me to where the truth is seen.*
> *Receipt of paper lost in the fray,*
> *Come forth now and show me the way.*

I WASN'T sure what to expect, but it wasn't this sensation of clarity. As if I didn't have a will of my own, I walked around the desk and opened a drawer that contained some file folders and a lot of haphazardly placed paper. Something beyond my control caused my hand to dig into the mess and pull out one piece of paper.

I blinked. "Are you kidding me? It worked. This is it!"

I wasn't sure what I was more excited about—finding the receipt or the fact my spell worked.

Nash stepped over to me and lifted the receipt from my fingers. It must have looked as if I wouldn't let it go.

"Well, I'll be. Good job, Glinda."

I smiled. "Thank you."

I blew out the candles and then cleaned up.

"I'll call Steve and tell him we found the receipt," Nash said.

"Let's hope Jaxson can figure out who sent the book. Though it might not do a lot of good unless Alistair or Katie were the ones who sent it to him."

"Agreed."

After we made sure things were more or less the way we found them, we returned to the sheriff's office. Steve, Jaxson, Iggy, and yes, Hugo, arrived a few minutes later since Harold lived on the outskirts of town.

"Let me make a copy of the receipt," Steve said.

Nash handed it to him.

Jaxson leaned over. "Was there a company name on the receipt?"

"There was, but it didn't tell me anything." And no, I didn't expect it to be called the Evergreen Company or something obvious.

"I'll see what I can find out," Jaxson said.

Steve returned, handed Jaxson a copy, and sat down. "Suppose Jaxson is able to trace the book back to one of our suspects? Any idea how to prove this person actually put a spell on it?"

I had been thinking a lot about how we were going to prove the killer was guilty. "I have an idea."

"Tell me," Steve said.

"This is a far-fetched analogy, but if you threw a grenade at someone, what would be your worst fear?" I asked.

"That they'd throw it right back at me," Steve said as if the answer was obvious.

"Correct. So what if we do the same with the book?"

Steve looked over at Nash, probably trying to wonder if what I was suggesting was even legal. "You mean give the book back to the person who we believe is the sorcerer?"

"Exactly. I am aware that the book could kill the person, but with the short exposure, the worst case would be that the person becomes ill for a bit."

"I don't think mailing it to our suspect would be smart. It might endanger too many people at the post office," Steve said.

I had thought of that. "It wouldn't go through the post office for that very reason. We would wrap it in brown packaging paper, put a few stamps on it, and place it on, say, Katie's doorstep—or whoever we believe is the killer."

"If we do this, we better be darn sure who the guilty party is," he said.

"Of course," I assured him.

CHAPTER 18

"I have an idea," Jaxson said.

"What's that?" I asked Jaxson.

"Let's assume we place the package on the killer's doorstep. What if Genevieve and Hugo cloaked themselves and watch to see whether the person takes the package inside his or her house?"

"I think most people would take it inside," Steve said.

"Okay. For the sake of argument, let's say we believe that Katie Altman is the killer. Once she opens the package, I'd love to see her reaction. If she's guilty of having placed the spell on the book in the first place, I'm betting she will call her uncle to see what he thinks she should do."

Steve leaned back in his chair. "I like it, except it doesn't provide a lot of proof other than what Genevieve can tell us about Katie's reaction. It would be hearsay."

"Then we record her." Jaxson held up a hand. "I realize that putting surveillance cameras pointed at her house—as well as inside her house—isn't legal, but you won't be trying her in a regular court. Humans don't believe in spells and such."

"I'll grant you that," the sheriff said.

Iggy pranced to the middle of the table. "You know what would be really cool?"

"What would be cool?" I repeated the question for Nash's sake.

"You could put a note inside the box saying it was from Harold Hastings." Iggy spun around. "I bet she'd freak over that."

I chuckled. "I think anyone would freak if they received a package from the deceased. Besides, I don't think anyone would really believe a note came from a dead person."

He waddled up to me. "You believed it when those ghosts at your birthday party visited you."

He had a point. "True. Okay. We could claim that Harold sent it to her before he died."

"I could take the package to the post office at night, grab a date stamp, and date it for the day before he died," Genevieve said. "Of course, I'd be cloaked."

"That sounds good," Steve said. "Jaxson, can I count on you to install the devices in and around both houses?"

"Absolutely."

"Hugo says he can help," Iggy said.

I had no idea that our resident gargoyle shifter knew anything about electronics. "What would be even better is if he could teleport Jaxson inside Katie's house while she's at work." I looked at Steve and then Nash to make sure they were on board with Katie being the possible guilty party. "We probably should do the same at Alistair's house. No telling if his niece will go over there with the book. They might even try to figure out a way to remove the spell."

"That would be helpful," Steve said.

"It would."

"Nash, how about you go with Jaxson to buy the needed equipment and then figure out a time to install it at both houses?" Steve said. "Hugo can help get you both inside at the appropriate time. If we're wrong, and Katie is excited about the gift, we'll have to regroup." Steve turned to Genevieve. "I'll put you in charge of removing the gift when you can, if Katie wants to keep it."

She saluted Steve. "Leave it to me."

"Genevieve, can you and Hugo be responsible for wrapping the gift and delivering it?" I asked.

"Sure. Maybe you can stop at the store to find a card that would make Katie believe it really came from Harold," she said.

"I can do that. I'll ask Bertha to help me—assuming she's at the store. She seemed to know him fairly well."

"Keep it simple," Steve said. "We don't want Katie to become suspicious."

I thought about asking his son, but that might complicate matters. "Got it."

While Nash and Jaxson took off to do their electronic surveillance purchase, I carried Iggy and went with Genevieve and Hugo back to the store. I imagined it seemed odd to them to move from one place to another by walking.

Andorra was manning the counter again, but this time, Bertha had returned from wherever and was straightening the shelves. Good. I handed Iggy to Hugo. "I'm going to speak with Bertha."

"Okay." Iggy seemed perfectly content to be with his friend.

I walked over to Bertha. "Hey."

She looked up and smiled. "I hear you've been busy."

"You could say that." I asked her to keep our conversation between us before I explained our plan. If we'd overlooked something, she might be able to spot it.

"What a shame if turns out that Katie is involved. She's always seemed so nice," Bertha said.

"I bet she is nice, except where it involves Harold. I don't blame her for being upset. After all, if we are to believe Harold's son, Harold erased his son's memory of her."

"I hope that's not true."

Anything was possible. "That's why we need proof."

I explained our plan. "Do you have a card that would look like something Harold would have sent? Let's assume that he doesn't realize she is Katie Altman, the woman he wanted erased from his son's memory."

"As a matter of fact, Harold has purchased a few cards from us. Come with me. We'll find a good one for you."

It didn't take long to find one that I thought would pass. "Now, I need to know what his handwriting looks like. Any ideas?"

"None, but I bet there is something in his house or store that is handwritten," Bertha said.

I smiled. "And I know just the person to find it. Thank you."

"Good luck."

I headed to the back room to find Genevieve. "Hey, I could use your help."

She pumped a fist. I had the sense she loved to be useful. I explained that I needed a sample of Harold's handwriting in order to write a message in the card.

She turned to Hugo. "How about you check his house, and I'll take the store." Hugo nodded. "We'll be right back."

True to their word, they returned less than ten minutes later with a few samples of his handwriting. Considering his home was rather messy—or so Jaxson reported—I was not expecting such good penmanship.

The only person I knew who could copy a person's handwriting was Penny. "I'm going to The Tiki Hut where Penny is working to see if she can do her magic on this note. When

I'm done, I'll give it back so you guys can put the card with the book. Okay?"

"Not a problem. When you return, we'll package the book to look like Harold sent it. We'll have to wait until after the post office closes before I sneak in and do my thing."

I chuckled. "I can't imagine what a postal worker would do if they saw the machine that prints the price move with no one around."

She smiled. "Exactly."

With the card and sample of Harold's handwriting, I crossed the street to my Aunt Fern's restaurant where Penny would be working. When I stepped inside, Aunt Fern was cashing someone out. I spotted Penny taking someone's order, so I went over to my aunt.

"This is a nice surprise," she said.

I looked around. "Believe it or not, I miss working here. Not that I would give up what Jaxson and I do, but I like interacting with the people."

"That's why I do it. I can't imagine not chatting with everyone, even if they are just passing through. So what brings you here?" my aunt asked.

I explained our plan. "I need Penny's help to write the note."

"I've seen her work. She's good."

As soon as Penny took care of her customer, I headed over to her. "Come to help out?"

"Don't you wish? Only kidding. I do miss this sometimes."

"Not that I don't love seeing you, but I'm sensing you need my help. Please say yes."

I smiled. "I do."

I told her what I needed. "We'll have to brainstorm what to say, but I have samples of his handwriting."

"Let's sit at this empty table." Penny studied the samples.

"This should be fairly easy. I've learned that the less said is better."

"Meaning, we should say: To Esmeralda, From Harold?"

"Didn't you say that Dolly told you Esmeralda—or rather Katie—was upset that he sold the flower book out from under her?"

"Yes."

"Then we address that. But I'll make it simple," Penny said.

"Perfect." Penny was better at what to say than I was.

With care, she crafted an amazing replica of Harold's handwriting. "There. I can't imagine anyone would question it."

"You are the best," I said. "I know you have to get back to work."

"Keep me posted."

"I will." Once I said goodbye to Aunt Fern, I returned with the card to the Hex and Bones and gave it to Genevieve.

"I can't wait to see how Katie reacts." She lifted a finger. "By the way, Hugo is with Jaxson and Nash right now getting them into and out of Katie and then Alistair's house so they can to do the installation work."

"Great," I said.

On my way back to the office, I texted Jaxson to see what his status was. He returned my text, saying they'd be done in about three hours.

I think the hardest part of being an amateur detective was waiting for something to happen. I couldn't be positive Katie had put the spell on the book, but she was the most likely candidate.

Jaxson returned to the office a little before dinner. "All done," he announced. "Thank goodness for Hugo. It made getting in and out rather easy. Hugo motioned that on the off chance either Katie or Alistair were to return home unexpectantly, he would grab our arms and make us invisible. Thankfully, that didn't happen."

"Good thing. Genevieve plans to go to the post office tonight once they gift wrap the book. Tomorrow, after Katie leaves for work, they will put the package on her doorstep," I said.

"This should be interesting," Jaxson said. "Now I need to do some research on that receipt. It might not be needed, but it won't hurt to find out where Harold got the book."

THE NEXT EVENING, Jaxson and I, along with Penny, Steve, and Nash, were in the sheriff's conference room huddled around the four portable television screens. Even though Nash and Jaxson had hidden cameras both inside and around both houses, Genevieve and Hugo said they would make a video of what went on inside the house as a backup. The fact neither Katie nor Alistair would have any idea they were being watched would make it all the more exciting.

The front door to Katie's house opened, and she stepped inside. "Here we go!" I said.

She carried the package into the kitchen and placed it on the counter. I was surprised she didn't even look at the address before she ripped it open. To be honest, it was what I would have done.

"Do you think she can feel the spell on the book?" Steve asked.

"I couldn't sense anything when Genevieve found it at the professor's house. Since it took a while for Harold to fall ill, it must be some kind of slow-acting spell," I said.

I sat on pins and needles waiting for Katie to figure out what we'd sent her. When she found the note and read it, her hands stilled. Only then did she check the date on the front. Good thing Genevieve had pre-dated it to the day before Harold's death.

Seemingly satisfied that a ghost hadn't sent it, Katie peeled back the paper. As soon as the cover was revealed, she jumped back. "What in the world? No, no, no."

I looked over at the others. Steve and Nash showed no emotion, but I could tell Penny was as excited as I was. So far, it seemed as if Katie was our witch in question.

She immediately pulled out her phone, and my gaze went to the screen that was in Alistair's living room. If he answered the phone, Hugo would have it covered.

Katie paced her living room while the phone in Alistair's house rang.

"Hey, Katie," Alistair said.

"You won't believe this. Before Harold died, he sent me *The Stone Enigma*."

"Isn't that the one that—"

"Yes, it is," she said.

"You have to get rid of it," her uncle said.

"How? I'm afraid to burn it. No telling what will happen."

Alistair had answered in another room but then walked into view of the hidden camera. "Bring it here. We'll come up with a plan. Do you know of a spell to remove your spell?"

CHAPTER 19

"I'm not sure," Katie said. "I have the spell I used, but I never thought to locate one to undo it."

"How long was the spell supposed to last?" her uncle asked.

Katie dragged a hand over her hair. "I don't know. I'm no expert in dark magic. I told you that."

"I know. Don't worry. Just come here, and we'll figure it out." Then Alistair hung up.

Bingo!

Steve and Nash just sat there, acting as if Katie hadn't just admitted to putting a spell on the book.

"Aren't you going to arrest her?" I asked.

"Yes, but let's see what happens once she takes the book to her uncle's place. At some point, we'll need Genevieve and Hugo to return the book to its safe hiding place."

I wish I had his patience. His plan had merit, however. "Fine."

It had been rather odd seeing—and hearing—both sides of the conversation. "If Katie has the spell written down, we need to find it. Levy said it would make it easier to locate an antidote if we know what we're dealing with."

Steve nodded. "When we bring her in, we can ask her about the spell. We might be able to bargain for it so you can do your purification spell on it."

Our sheriff was smart. "Thank you."

Steve pushed back his chair and stood. "Time for an arrest. I need Nash to come with me. Can one of you call me if the situation changes? I know Genevieve and Hugo can do their thing, but I'd like to know if something is going down before we get there."

"We can do that." I looked over at the screen. Katie was on her way out. "Just don't beat her there."

Steve seemed to swallow a smile. "This isn't my first rodeo, you know."

"Sorry."

Once he and Nash left, the three of us returned to watching the small television screens. It didn't take Katie long to arrive at her uncle's place. She must have been afraid of being followed or spotted, because she parked a few houses away from Alistair's place.

"Let's hope Katie and Alistair have a good solution for removing that curse," Penny said. "Otherwise, you'll have to do more magic, Glinda."

I'd been lucky to find the receipt. I wasn't so sure I could succeed again. I thought about asking Gertrude to do the spell, but I didn't want to expose someone of her advanced age to the cursed book.

"Look," Jaxson said nudging me. "Steve and Nash have arrived."

He knocked on Alistair's door, and Alistair looked through the peephole. "It's the sheriff and the deputy. They can't know anything, can they?" he asked his niece.

It was at that moment that both Genevieve and Hugo

uncloaked themselves. She must have followed Katie—or teleported straight from Katie's house to Alistair's.

Both Katie and Alistair looked rather surprised. "Who are you?" he asked.

"Hugo and I have been videotaping you. We know Katie killed Harold by putting a spell on *The Enigma Stone*, which is a fake, by the way."

The moment Alistair stepped toward Genevieve, Hugo was right there to contain him.

"Let me go," Alistair protested.

Hugo released him, but he stood next to Alistair to make sure he didn't hurt Genevieve, though she could just have cloaked herself and moved away.

Steve and Nash came inside. "Katie and Alistair, you are both under arrest for the murder of Harold Hastings," Steve said. "I would read you your rights, but you won't be tried in a human court. Rather, those with magical abilities will judge you."

"I didn't do anything," Alistair said.

"Uh-huh." Steve knew that wasn't true.

"You don't have any idea what a horrible man Harold was," Katie proclaimed.

"That may be, but you killed him and caused harm to someone else who got a hold of this book."

Katie stilled and then looked around. "You set me up. Harold never sent me this book then, did he?"

"No, he didn't. Come on."

"Talk to Harold's son, Charles," Katie said. "We were engaged until Harold erased Charles' memory of me. Do you know what that was like?"

"I can't imagine," Steve said.

Steve slipped handcuffs on both of them. He then escorted Katie and Alistair outside.

I leaned back in my seat. In a flash, both Genevieve and

Hugo appeared. "How did we do?" Genevieve said with a grin.

"You two were amazing. Thank you," I said. "I have one more favor."

"Anything."

"You have the book, right?" I asked.

"Not with us. We stored it where no one will be hurt—for now."

Since Genevieve was able to retrieve it so quickly, it wasn't as if she buried it one hundred feet in the ground. "I'd like to do a purification spell on the book. I know it's not an original, but someone like Priscilla Primm could use it for research."

"You know of such a spell?" Genevieve asked.

"No, but if you could find the original spell at Katie's house, we might be able to reverse-engineer it." That wasn't how it worked, but I think she understood.

"I'll see what I can find," she said.

I suppose if she couldn't find it, I could do another location spell like I did for the receipt.

Jaxson turned to Hugo. "Do you think you could help me remove the cameras from both houses?"

Hugo nodded. Then Genevieve, Hugo, and Jaxson stepped out of the glass-enclosed conference room, stood behind a wall, and then disappeared.

I would have asked to go with her, but I wasn't about to leave Penny all alone.

"If you get the spell and are able to remove it, Katie will have nothing to bargain with," Penny said.

"True. I feel sorry for her, but her anger caused the death of a man. Whether he was rotten as many say, I don't know, but it seemed as if he was trying to change his ways once he moved here," I said.

"I get it."

We didn't have to wait long for Genevieve to return. Thankfully, she was behind the wall when she reappeared. She entered the glass-enclosed room smiling, waving a piece of paper. "Success."

She handed me the paper. "Awesome. Thank you for finding this."

Penny leaned over my shoulder and read the spell. "It doesn't seem that evil."

"Did you read the part about weakening the person?" It didn't guarantee they would die, but Harold was old.

"I was focusing on the part where it made the person paranoid. Maybe the person was supposed to put an end to their life," she said.

"That could explain why he was under the pew. Harold could have imagined all sorts of things, including his son, Joseph, Alistair, or anyone else he'd harmed was after him."

"That makes sense."

"Before the group returns, how about we head over to Gertrude's to see if she knows how to reverse the spell?" I asked.

Penny smiled. "I'd love to visit with the old lady."

I stood. "We'll have to pick up Iggy. He'd be fit to be tied if we didn't let him visit with us."

"What about me?" Genevieve asked.

"Would you mind staying here? Steve and Nash might need you to do something—like communicate with Hugo."

"Sure."

She sounded disappointed, but that couldn't be helped. Penny and I crossed the street. She climbed into my car, while I went inside our apartment to get Iggy.

"How did it go?" he asked. I was pleased he wasn't angry that he hadn't come with us.

As we went back outside, I gave him a brief rundown.

"I knew it was Katie from the get-go," Iggy said.

"Did you now? What gave it away?" His responses were rarely based on fact, but I had learned not to dismiss his intuition.

"If someone erased your memory of me, I'd want to hurt them too."

"Iggy, retaliation is a bad thing," I said. Secretly, I was happy he thought enough of me to want to get back at someone.

When we reached the car, I slid in, handed Iggy to Penny, and started the engine.

"Hi there, little guy," she said.

"I haven't seen you in a while," Iggy told her.

"That's not true. You see me every time you come downstairs to speak with Fern," Penny said.

"I know, but we don't chat. You're always busy."

"True." She looked over at me. "Do you think Gertrude will know a spell off the top of her head?" Penny asked.

"I don't know, but if she's stumped, she'll call Levy. Now that we have the dark spell, it should be a lot easier."

Hopefully, Gertrude would be home. I probably should have called. When I pulled into her driveway, her car was there thank goodness. We piled out and went to the front door. I didn't even have to knock, because Gertrude answered before I had the chance.

"Well, this is a new record," she said. "Twice in a week. Come in, ladies. Nice to see you again, Penny."

"You too."

"And my favorite familiar joined you. Wonderful! Can I get you ladies something to drink?"

I wasn't really thirsty, but I knew Gertrude loved playing hostess. "Tea or coffee would be fine."

"For me also," Penny said.

While Gertrude fixed us drinks, I placed the paper with the spell on the coffee table and then we sat on the sofa.

She returned and handed us our drinks. "Now tell me what you need help with."

I explained how Esmeralda, or rather, Katie, admitted to putting a dark spell on a book that eventually killed Harold. "Here is the spell that Genevieve located in Katie's house. We're hoping you can help us with a purification spell. We don't want anyone else becoming ill or dying."

"Certainly not." She stood and walked over to a bookcase. "I remember reading something about that." She pulled down three large books and carried them over. "It should be in one of these."

She handed us each a book. "What are we looking for exactly?" Penny asked.

"You should see the word purification in the title."

"That seems easy enough".

For the next hour, we poured over the books. When I turned the page, I stilled. "I think I found it."

Gertrude motioned for me to show her. I handed her the book.

She read it over. "This is perfect, and the ingredients are easy to come by."

When she gave it back to me, I studied the instructions. "It says the white candle represents purity, healing, and positive energy. That makes sense we'd need that."

Penny tapped the page. "Rosemary is known for its protective and purifying powers. It says it can aid in removing dark energies. That is also perfect."

"The clear quartz crystal might be the hardest ingredient to find," I said.

"Nonsense," Gertrude snorted. "Penny, head over to my desk and look in the top drawer. You'll find exactly what you ladies need. Mind you, I'd like it back."

"Of course," I told her. I knew that the crystal would

dispel the negative energy and help restore clarity and balance.

The other ingredients of lavender, bay leaf, and salt were also known for their purifying properties. "Why do you think we need paper?" I asked.

"I imagine it will represent the book you are trying to cleanse," she said.

"That makes sense too." I looked over at Penny. "Ready to do this?"

"I am."

"I suggest you set up everything first and then have Genevieve deliver the book. You don't want too much exposure to it," Gertrude said.

I always took all of her warnings seriously. "I will. And thank you."

"Just make sure that book never hurts anyone again."

"Glinda, you should copy down the instructions. The order is important," Penny reminded me.

"Good idea."

Gertrude gave me some paper, and I copied down the instructions. Once done, I hugged Gertrude. "You are the best."

"You silly girl. Go and take away that curse. Do me proud."

I smiled. "I will. Come on, Iggy. Say goodbye to Gertrude."

He crawled up her arm and kissed her on the cheek like usual. Then he waddled over to me. I picked him up. "Let's do this."

CHAPTER 20

Not wanting Iggy to be exposed to any dark spell, I took him back to the apartment. While there, I gathered some bay leaves, salt, a few white candles that I had, and a small plate. I then carefully gathered the rest of the tools for the spell. "I'll be back shortly. If Jaxson comes home, tell him I'm at Hex and Bones with Penny trying to remove the spell."

"I'll need lettuce when you get back."

His quirky demand made me chuckle. "Why? Because remembering all the instructions uses up a lot of mental energy?"

"Make fun of my need to eat and see if I help solve any more crimes." Iggy lifted his snout, his eyes glinting playfully.

I suppressed a laugh. "Yes, sir."

I quickly returned to the backroom of the Hex and Bones, the air thick with a sense of anticipation. Genevieve was back.

"How did it go?" I asked her, my voice a hushed whisper as if the very walls could carry our secrets.

She shrugged. "Both are at the station protesting their innocence. It didn't seem to matter that we had videos of them.

They said the recordings were illegal, but Steve reminded them once more that they would be tried in a court of their peers—and not in the normal legal system. They weren't pleased."

"I imagine not. Where's Hugo?" I inquired, my eyes flickering to the shadowed corners of the room, thinking he might have cloaked himself.

"After he and Jaxson removed the cameras from both houses, Hugo went to the station for sentry duty. No telling what those two can do. Even if they can cloak themselves, Hugo will know if they are still there."

"Steve should hire him to be at the sheriff's department permanently," I mused, imagining the gargoyle's imposing presence adding an extra layer of security.

"I imagine he'd like that, but then I'd have to go over there to recharge him, so to speak." Genevieve's voice carried a touch of amusement.

I'd never fully comprehended the intricacies of Hugo's existence nor the nuances of his interactions with Genevieve. "When Hugo—or you—are in your gargoyle form, you are aware of what's going on?"

"Of course," she replied, her gaze momentarily distant as if recalling past moments in their unique companionship.

"You know, if Hugo wanted to, he could sit in the corner in his gargoyle form and then change when needed," I suggested.

"That would be great, but only if he's guarding a witch or a warlock. A regular human would think he was seeing things if Hugo suddenly changed form." She laughed. "Come to think of it, that has happened a time or two when we were not paying attention."

"That poor person." As much as I loved to chit-chat, I needed to do this spell. "Once I set up for the spell, can you bring the book here?" I asked Genevieve.

"Just tell me when."

"Do you mind if I use that table over there?" I gestured to a corner of the room.

"Sure," she said.

She and Penny cleared off some of the boxes and moved the table. I then sat down and lit my white candles. Next, I arranged the rosemary, Gertrude's clear quartz crystal, lavender, and the bay leaf on the small plate. The next step required me to hold the piece of paper in my hands to symbolize the book. It was time to start. "I'm ready."

"Be right back," Genevieve said.

It only seemed like seconds before Genevieve returned with the book. My body tensed, knowing what evil it possessed. "Can you sense the evil?" I asked Genevieve.

"Yes. I think it's actually getting stronger."

I didn't want to hear that. "Okay, please put the book in front of me."

I ripped the piece of paper that contained both the spell and the instructions into two pieces. "Penny, can you help me with the instructions while I concentrate on the spell?"

"Of course."

Holding the piece of paper in my hands, I looked over at Penny. "What's the first step?"

The candles flickered, casting shadows upon the walls. The fragrance of bay leaves and lavender mingled in the air, creating a sense of serenity amid the anticipation that hung like a veil.

"Recite the spell with conviction and focus, channeling your intention into words," she said.

"That should be easy. Or not." I wasn't sure I was up for this task, but I had to try. I inhaled and tried to clear my mind. I then began.

"Wait!" Penny said. "As you recite the spell, gently pass the paper through the smoke of the candle to purify it. Thank goodness I caught that."

"I got this."

As calmly as I could, I spoke the words of the spell, trying hard to pronounce each one with reverence and intent. The atmosphere seemed to shimmer with a subtle energy as if the very air was responding to the ancient incantation.

"By pages turned and secrets penned,
A darkened curse we now amend.
From book's embrace, let evil part,
Release its grip, restore the heart.
Gentle winds and moonlit skies,
Unravel the curse that twists and lies.
With magic's touch and whispered plea,
Set this book and its keeper free.
From shadows deep, I now implore,
Reverse the spell, forevermore.
By charm and wit, the darkness break,
Let goodness thrive, for love's sweet sake.
Eyes of light and laughter's bloom,
Banish the darkness, lift the gloom.
With every word, with every line,
Undo the curse, let light entwine.
As I speak, so shall it be,
From darkened spell, this book is free."

"Good job," Penny said. "Now extinguish the candle and bury the remnants of the paper in the earth as a way to ground the energy."

"We have to bury it?" I asked.

"That's what it says," Penny told me.

Genevieve walked over and removed it from my fingers. "Leave it to me."

"Before you go," Penny said. "We're supposed to put the big book in a place where it can absorb positive energy and light."

Genevieve smiled. "I know the perfect place. I'll place it on the roof of the church where Hugo and I used to sit. I can't think of a better place than that."

"I like it, but I wonder how long it will take before the spell is totally gone?" I asked.

"I'll keep checking. I'll know when it's good to go." Genevieve picked up the hopefully spell-free book and disappeared.

I leaned back in my seat. "Is it really over?" I asked.

"I think so. The next step is up to the courts to decide what crime to charge Katie and Alistair. If it were being held in our court of law, they'd get off scot-free since regular people would never believe someone could put a curse on a book."

I smiled. "You are right about that. I'm so happy we have Steve and Nash in charge. They actually believe in magic."

"Well, it helps that Nash is a werewolf—or should I say he used to be one since he doesn't shift anymore."

"That we know of." I pushed back my chair and gathered my candle, dish, and the other ingredients. "I can't thank you enough for helping."

"Are you kidding? I loved being involved, though I didn't do much," Penny said. "As much as I would love to stick around, I need to get back to Tommy."

"I can't believe he's nine already. Where did the time go?"

"Tell me about it." Penny hugged me goodbye and then left.

Genevieve returned. "All done. I didn't sense the spell, but we'll wait a few days to be sure."

"I appreciate it. I'm going to head on back. I imagine Jaxson will be home, and Iggy will be asking way too many questions."

"No doubt."

After I said goodbye to Andorra and Bertha, I crossed the street to our apartment. Sure enough, Jaxson was there with Iggy next to him.

"Did the spell work?" Iggy asked.

"I believe so. Genevieve said she can't detect any evil."

Jaxson stood and took the items out of my hands. He set them on the coffee table and hugged me. "I'm proud of you."

I leaned back. "Why is that?"

"You're usually hesitant to do spells since you're afraid of messing them up, yet you did it anyway."

I wasn't that bad. Or was I? "Well, thank you."

He lifted a finger. "Before I forget, I need to tell you that I was able to trace the origin on the book receipt."

"And?"

"It came from a company located in none other than Oakfield, Florida," he said.

"Don't tell me that company was where either Alistair or Katie worked."

He smiled. "It was Alistair's old company. He must have asked someone there to mail it."

"That kind of seals Alistair's fate. He might not have put the spell on the book, but he was involved in other ways."

"I agree. Before you ask, I sent all of the information to Steve already. He sounded quite pleased to have something concrete."

"That's wonderful." My stomach grumbled. "I'm starving, by the way. Anyone interested in some Tiki Hut food?"

"Me!" Iggy proclaimed.

I laughed. "You know what comes next, don't you?" I asked Jaxson.

"Of course. I need to make an honest woman out of you."

"Exactly. There are some details we have to work out."

"Then let's do that!"

Three days later

"Knock, knock, can I come in?" Jaxson's voice echoed through the door.

I finished checking my appearance. "Of course, you can."

He stepped into the room. "Sweet. I thought I wasn't supposed to see the bride-to-be before the wedding."

Amusement tugged at my lips. "Too late for that. You've already seen me."

Drawing nearer, he pulled me into an affectionate embrace. "You're even more beautiful than the first time I saw you walk down the aisle." His words were sincere and tender. I so loved this man.

Because I wasn't totally comfortable in my own skin, I dismissed his compliment with a light chuckle. "You're silly."

A determined glint lit up his eyes. "No. I'm serious. I think I was a little too nervous to appreciate things the first time. Now, there will just be the family."

I nodded in agreement. "And Andorra and Penny." A fleeting sadness accompanied my words, thinking of those who couldn't be here. "I wish Gertrude had accepted."

"I think she knew we wanted to keep it small. If she'd said yes, then we'd have to ask Levy, and before you know it, we're back to half the town being there."

"You're right. And may I say you look amazing in your tux?"

"Why thank you. I did have to promise Iggy that he could eat the hibiscus when we were done."

I laughed. We had to bribe him with something in order to get him to wear the ring around his neck instead of carrying it in his mouth.

"Ready, my soon-to-be wife?" Jaxson held out his arm.

"More than ready."

Iggy was on the sofa, not looking all that happy wearing the blue ribbon. "Come on, mister. Time to shine."

"I hope the ceremony is short. I feel ridiculous carrying the ring this way."

"I think you look cute."

Jaxson grabbed him, and the three of us went downstairs. This time, our parents, Aunt Fern, and the others were meeting us at the church, so Jaxson drove.

When we arrived, the front of the church was back to normal. I had to remind myself that we were here for legal purposes only since we'd already said our vows. However, we had chosen to let the minister recreate the ceremony, treating this as our first time.

Jaxson cut the engine and walked around to my side. "Shall we?"

He escorted me inside the church. To my surprise, an organist was playing the wedding march again. No doubt, Aunt Fern had requested it.

When we walked down the aisle, Jaxson carried Iggy. We weren't taking any chances with losing the ring again. Those who were there, were seated in the first few rows. There was no need to ask our wedding party to dress up again.

Penny waved and grinned as Jaxson and I stepped onto the altar.

The minister's voice resonated through the sacred space as he spoke the words that would bind us. We repeated our vows, each promise carrying the weight of our shared journey.

With a playful twinkle in his eye, Jaxson handed Iggy to me, the iguana an unexpected yet cherished part of our union. As the minister concluded his words, I set Iggy on the floor between us, and Jaxson slipped the ring onto my finger, sealing our commitment.

After a few more words, the minister announced that Jaxson could kiss me. The moment his lips met mine, time seemed to stand still, the world narrowing down to this tangible connection. A soft tap on my leg, courtesy of Iggy, broke the spell, eliciting laughter from our guests.

The official signing of the papers followed, which was the final step to solidifying our union. In the company of family and friends, we gathered together, our hands and hearts intertwined.

Once the ceremony came to a close, Jaxson's parents approached us and handed Jaxson an envelope. "What's this?" he asked.

Maddie's smile held warmth and goodwill. "Your dad and I thought you and Glinda should have a proper honeymoon, so here are two plane tickets and hotel reservations to Antigua in the Caribbean."

Surprise and gratitude washed over me. The image of a Caribbean escape painted a vivid picture in my mind. "That is so generous of you."

Maddie's eyes twinkled. "Promise me that if you find a dead body, leave it to the authorities to deal with it."

"I promise," I assured them.

As the warmth of love and contentment enveloped me, I knew that this was a moment to cherish. Jaxson's arm encircled my waist. We exchanged glances, recognizing that our shared journey was just beginning.

"Ready to chow, Mrs. Harrison?" Jaxson's playful question

drew me from my thoughts, reminding me of the celebrations yet to come.

"Of course," I responded, my heart brimming with happiness. Glancing around for Iggy, I couldn't help but chuckle. "Now, where is that scoundrel?"

Iggy's head peeked out from beneath a pew. "All clear. We're good to go."

"Glad to hear it."

With a sense of anticipation and the promise of new beginnings, Jaxson and I stepped out of the church, our hearts aligned, and our future waiting to unfold.

Things would never be dull in Witch's Cove.

Don't forget to sign up for my Cozy Mystery newsletter to learn about my discounts and upcoming releases. If you prefer to only receive notices regarding my releases, follow me on BookBub.

THE END

ABOUT THE AUTHOR

Love it HOT and STEAMY? Sign up for my newsletter and receive MONTANA DESIRE for FREE. Click here

OR Are you a fan of quirky PARANORMAL COZY MYSTERIES? Sign up for this newsletter. Click Here

Not only do I love to read, write, and dream, I'm an extrovert. I enjoy being around people and am always trying to understand what makes them tick. Not only must my romance books have a happily ever after, I need characters I can relate to. My men are wonderful, dynamic, smart, strong, and the best lovers in the world (of course).

My Paranormal Cozy Mysteries are where I let my imagination run wild with witches and a talking pink iguana who believes he's a real sleuth.

I believe I am the luckiest woman. I do what I love and I have a wonderful, supportive husband, who happens to be hot!

Fun facts about me
(1) I'm a math nerd who loves spreadsheets. Give me numbers and I'll find a pattern.
(2) I live on a Costa Rica beach!
(3) I also like to exercise. Yes, I know I'm odd.

I love hearing from readers either on FB or via email (hint, hint).

Social Media Sites

Website: www.velladay.com
FB: www.facebook.com/vella.day.90
Twitter: velladay4
Gmail: velladayauthor@gmail.com
Tiktok: Velladayauthor1
Bookbub: https://www.bookbub.com/authors/vella-day

ALSO BY VELLA DAY

THE TIME TRAVEL TALISMAN COZY MYSTERY (Cozy Mystery)

The Knitting Conundrum (book 1)

The Knitting Dilemma (book 2)

The Knitting Enigma (book 3)

The Knitting Quandary (book 4)

A WITCH'S COVE MYSTERY (Paranormal Cozy Mystery)

PINK Is The New Black (book 1)

A PINK Potion Gone Wrong (book 2)

The Mystery of the PINK Aura (book 3)

Box Set (books 1-3)

Sleuthing In The PINK (book 4)

Not in The PINK (book 5)

Gone in the PINK of an Eye (book 6)

Box Set (books 4-6)

The PINK Pumpkin Party (book 7)

Mistletoe with a PINK Bow (book 8)

The Magical PINK Pendant (book 9)

Box Set (books 7-9)

The Poisoned PINK Punch (book 10)

PINK Smoke and Mirrors (book 11)

Broomsticks and PINK Gumdrops (book 12)

Box Set (books 10-12)

Knotted Up In PINK Yarn (book 13)

Ghosts and PINK Candles (book 14)

Pilfered PINK Pearls (book 15)

Box Set (books 13-15)

The Case of the Stolen PINK Tombstone (book 16)

The PINK Christmas Cookie Caper (book 17)

PINK Moon Rising (book 18)

Box set(books 16-18)

The PINK Wedding Dress Whodunit (book 19)

SILVER LAKE SERIES (3 OF THEM)
A TASTE OF SILVER LAKE
Weres and Witches Box Set (books 1-2)
Hidden Realms Box Set (books 1-2)
Goddesses of Destiny Box Set (books 1-2)

(1). **HIDDEN REALMS OF SILVER LAKE** (Paranormal Romance)

Awakened By Flames (book 1)

Seduced By Flames (book 2)

Box Set (books 1-2)

Kissed By Flames (book 3)

Destiny In Flames (book 4)

Box Set (books 3-4)

Passionate Flames (book 5)

Ignited By Flames (book 6)

Box Set (books 5-6)

Touched By Flames (book 7)

Bound By Flames (book 8)

Box set (books 7-8)

Fueled By Flames (book 9)

Scorched By Flames (book 10)

Box Set (books 9-10)

(2). **GODDESSES OF DESTINY** Paranormal Romance)

Slade (book 1)

Rafe (book 2)

Will (book 3)

Josh (book 4)

Jace (book 5)

Tanner (book 6)

(3). **WERES AND WITCHES OF SILVER LAKE** (Paranormal Romance)

A Magical Shift (book 1)

Catching Her Bear (book 2)

Surge of Magic (book 3)

The Bear's Forbidden Wolf (book 4)

Box Set (books 1-4)

Her Reluctant Bear (book 5)

Freeing His Tiger (book 6)

Protecting His Wolf (book 7)

Waking His Bear (book 8)

Box Set (books 5-8)

Melting Her Wolf's Heart (book 9)

Her Wolf's Guarded Heart (book 10)

His Rogue Bear (book 11)

Reawakening Their Bears (book 12)

Box Set (books 9-12)

OTHER PARANORMAL SERIES

PACK WARS (Paranormal Romance)
Training Their Mate (book 1)
Claiming Their Mate (book 2)
Rescuing Their Virgin Mate (book 3)
Box Set (books 1-3)
Loving Their Vixen Mate (book 4)
Fighting For Their Mate (book 5)
Enticing Their Mate (book 6)
Box Set (books 4-6)
Their Huntress Mate (book 7)
Craving Their Mate (book 8)

PACK WARS-THE GRANGERS
Meant for them (book 1)
Meant for wolves (book 2)
Meant for forever (book 3)
Meant for her (book 4)

HIDDEN HILLS SHIFTERS (Paranormal Romance)
An Unexpected Diversion (book 1)
Bare Instincts (book 2)
Shifting Destinies (book 3)
Embracing Fate (book 4)
Promises Unbroken (book 5)
Bare 'N Dirty (book 6)
Hidden Hills Shifters Complete Box Set (books 1-6)

CONTEMPORARY SERIES

MONTANA PROMISES (Full length contemporary Romance)

Promises of Mercy (book 1)

Foundations For Three (book 2)

Montana Fire (book 3)

Montana Promises Box Set (books 1-3)

Hart To Hart (Book 4)

Burning Seduction (Book 5)

Montana Promises Complete Box Set (books 1-5)

Novellas:

Montana Desire (book 1)

Awakening Passions (book 2)

PLEDGED TO PROTECT (contemporary romantic suspense)

From Panic To Passion (book 1)

From Danger To Desire (book 2)

From Terror To Temptation (book 3)

BURIED SERIES (contemporary romantic suspense)

Buried Alive (book 1)

Buried Secrets (book 2)

Buried Deep (book 3)

The Buried Series Complete Box Set (books 1-3)

A NASH MYSTERY (Contemporary Romance)

Sidearms and Silk(book 1)

Black Ops and Lingerie(book 2)

A Nash Mystery Box Set (books 1-2)

STARTER SETS (Romance)

Contemporary

Paranormal